THE VANISHING OF
FLIGHT 187

A JACK TALBOT THRILLER

MARC W SHAKO

This is a work of fiction. Names, characters, businesses, places, events and incidents are either the products of the author's imagination or used in a fictitious manner. Any resemblance to actual persons, living, dead, or undead, or actual events is purely coincidental.

The Vanishing of Flight 187 Copyright © Marc Wobschall 2020

This one's for you, Mum.

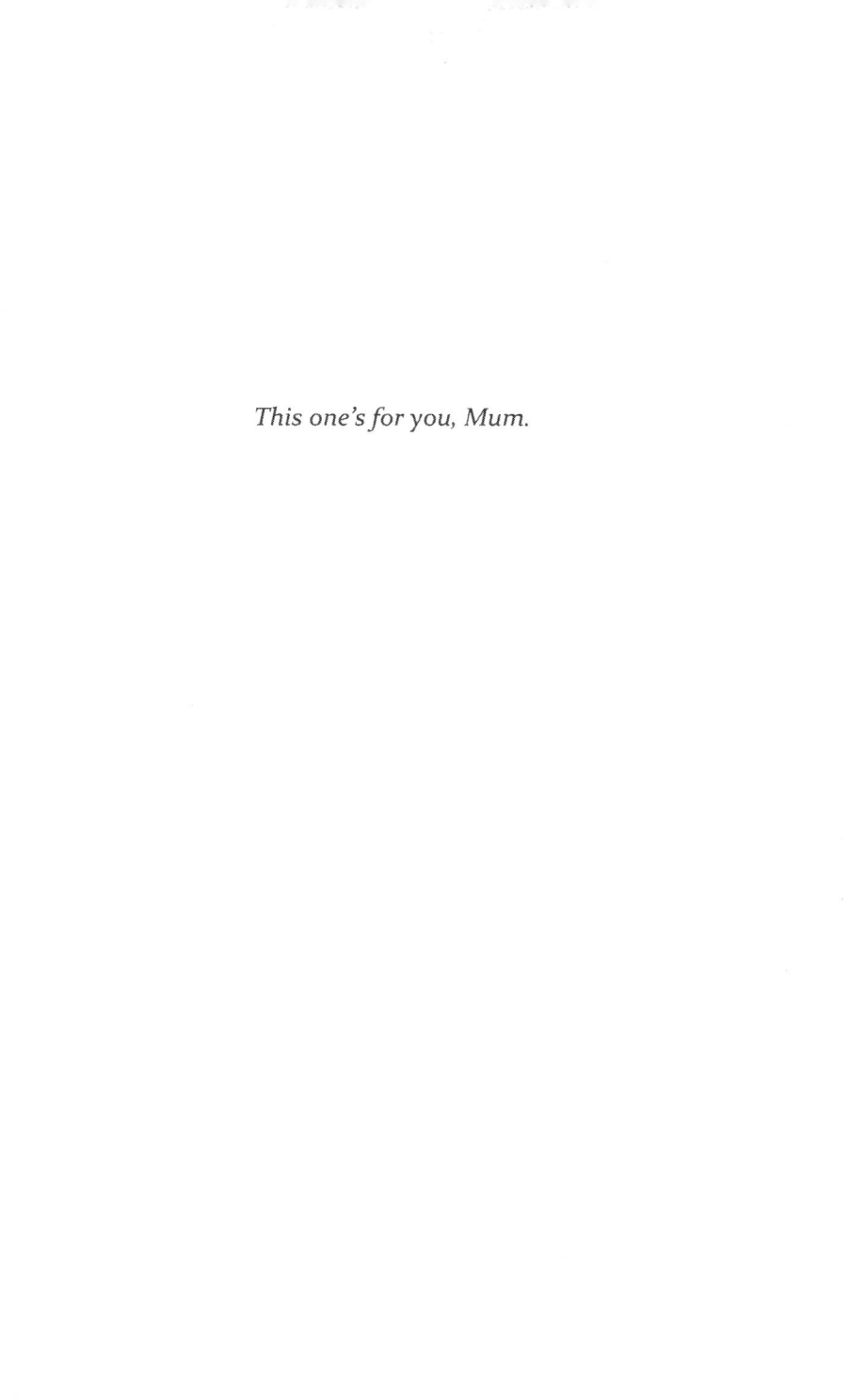

CHAPTER ONE

ADAM SHEPHERD WAVED a hand at a passing waiter and signalled it was time to pay. The waiter nodded and Adam drained his scotch.

The restaurant was still half full, and Adam wondered how these people all ate so late. Normally at this hour, he'd be in his office knee deep in paperwork, but tonight was different.

'Was everything to your satisfaction, sir?' the waiter asked placing the leather wallet on the table.

He thought about his steak being a little underdone, but it was hard to find somewhere that cooked steak exactly as he wanted. Better under than over. 'Excellent, thank you.' He smiled, handing over his card.

Outside, he glanced in the direction of the airport and the storm flickering behind it. He sighed as he climbed into his car, sitting in silence for a moment before the key went anywhere near the ignition.

'Happy Anniversary,' he said softly.

He wiped a solitary tear with a handkerchief and puffed out a breath of air, steadying his nerve and his hand. Before he started the engine, he grabbed his phone.

'I take it all is well?'

'As always,' his assistant replied.

'That's what I like to hear. Goodnight, Karen. Call me if anything comes up.'

He started the engine and set off. The closer he got to home the more the dread feeling crept that he'd spend another night battling insomnia.

Not that he wasn't tired. He'd been under no illusions about the amount of work running this new venture would bring, but now he'd laugh off what his past self would call stress. Although he had hoped he'd be spending more time on the golf course, not less, but it was what it was, and he wouldn't change it for anything. The profits were nice but like with any business it came with its own headaches. It wasn't just balancing the books that he had to worry about. Or insomnia.

In his fight with restlessness, he'd been trying a relaxation technique his therapist had told him to use, thinking in pictures, not words. He liked to imagine the fourteenth hole at the local links. Just a par four, but a long one. Tee up. Take the driver. A long straight drive and his ball was rolling to the end of the dogleg right. A nice walk along the fairway's gentle undulations. The breeze cooling him. The red flag gently fluttering on the green. The seven iron should do it from here. He was always asleep before he reached the green. It worked for him every time, he hoped tonight would be no exception.

2

Forty miles away, the automatic doors slid aside, and three

women burst into the terminal building, hit by bright lighting and the tail end of an announcement. Hearing your name mentioned over the intercom at the airport was never good. The oldest led the way with a sense of real purpose, which was odd only because she was the only one not dragging a small bag behind her.

'This way,' she ordered.

She skilfully manoeuvred between slower passengers, gritting her teeth and doing her best not to be angry. The only reason the other passengers were moving so slowly was that they had better organisational skills than her sister; she shouldn't blame them for arriving on time. It was always this way with Hannah. Late for everything. Luckily for Hannah, she'd been there to give her sister a much-needed boot up the backside. She'd become accustomed to her younger sister's tardiness, but now it was making Nicola late. She stopped dead and craned her neck to the departures board. Her head scanned left and right looking for the signs for gate 6.

'Here,' she said, imagining the faces her sister was making to Nicola behind her.

They could make as many faces as they liked once they'd been through passport control. The queue was thankfully short, around a dozen waiting in line. They'd make it. Just.

She turned to see Hannah who flicked a curl of her long flowing wavy hair over her shoulder. That hair. Hers was too straight and she could never do a thing with it.

'Got everything?' she said, aware that it had been the fourth time she'd asked since they'd left the house.

'Ruth, relax,' Hannah said.

'I'm just checking.'

'I'm twenty-seven, not twelve,' Hannah replied.

A dull growl of thunder rumbled from the distance. It was barely audible over the sounds of an announcement which sounded like Mr and Mrs Miller were later for their flight than Hannah was; Ruth glanced up briefly but diverted her gaze hoping not to draw Hannah's attention to it. It didn't work.

Hannah sighed, 'They'd better not cancel this flight too. I've already lost half a day's shopping.'

Ruth smiled and shook her head at her sister and thought about saying something but bit her lip. Hannah didn't want any more mothering, especially in front of her friend. Their trip was only for a few days, but it was an important one; leading a three-day training session to get the new European partners up to speed on a brand-new team. It must have meant a lot to the company to hold the training over the weekend and pay all involved double time, though the rumours of problems in Frankfurt left this as no surprise. Apparently German organisation is not what it once was. Hannah and Nicola seemed calmer than she was. They looked like they were looking forward to a break from the norm. The queue for the passport check in front was down to the last two: middle-aged businessmen, three sheets to the wind.

Ruth turned to Hannah. 'Well, have a safe flight and I'll see you in a couple of days.'

Nicola answered, 'We don't want to ruin your Sunday, we can take a taxi when we get back, it'll be fine.'

Hannah nudged her, 'Shush, Nix, we're on a free ride

here.'

All three smiled.

'It'll be fine. Hugs,' Ruth said, quickly hugging Nicola first before squeezing Hannah. 'Have a safe flight.'

'You've said that. We'll be fine. Won't we Nix?'

Nic smiled at Ruth, 'It's them I'd worry about.'

They were called forward and Ruth watched them go through security and waited for Hannah to wave before turning and leaving for the car park. She hated goodbyes.

3

Sean Cook watched the green arm sweep the radar display in the air traffic control tower. Through the window, flights queued ready for take-off as the latest outbound shrank into the night. His colleague Steve was already welcoming a flight of probably miserable holidaymakers back from Tenerife, but maybe some of them were like him and looking forward to getting home. It had been a long day. Uneventful, which is all you could ask for, but still, all he wanted now was a couple of cold ones, and to fall asleep in front of the telly. Air traffic was slowing as he neared the end of his shift. The next flight out was the Shepherd Airlines to Frankfurt. He had a soft spot for Shepherd. Local businessman done good. Relatively new airline, new fleet of aircraft, 100% safety record still intact.

'Shepherd one eight seven, destination Frankfurt as filed, climb initially flight level one four zero, seven three one seven on the squawk.'

'This is Shepherd one eight seven, our clear destination Frankfurt via flight plan route one four zero initially, seven three one seven on the squawk, Shepherd one eight seven and we have total passengers one seven five.'

He gave the instruction to taxi to the runway ready for take-off. One hundred and seventy-five souls aboard. The flight wasn't full despite it being a reschedule. Not full. Whenever he saw that the terrible thought entered his head that if he *were* to lose a flight... well, it could be much worse.

The pilots set the transponder to 7317 and were waiting for word to go. The lightning in the distance flickered like a faulty strip light.

'Shepherd one eight seven we are ready for departure.'

Sean checked the wind speed. 'Shepherd one eight seven, surface wind two six zero one three knots, you are cleared for take-off.'

Sean watched as the huge bird raced down the runway, speeds building until the wheels gently lifted from the smooth surface. He'd relax once they reached fourteen hundred feet. First hurdle cleared, chances of disaster reduced by 16%. That's how he thought of flights. Take-off and landing were the tricky parts. Sixteen per cent of incidents happening during take-off. Lots of room for human error, from him, the pilot, other pilots. The flight disappeared behind the roof of the tower.

Once they were up, the chances of disaster dropped significantly, until it was time to land. Sean glanced at the radar. Shepherd 187 was on its own and in the clear. Nothing around. Well, there was the storm raging off to the southeast, but that was too far away to be anything other than a fancy light show for the passengers, nothing that should cause concern for the pilots.

'Tower this is Shepherd one eight seven requesting change of altitude.'

Change of altitude? They were barely up. That would be a request once they'd been handed off to the control centre. He glanced at the radar. As far as he could tell, 187 was alone. There was nothing near them, unless they'd hit a pocket of turbulence he was unaware of... His eyes shifted back to the radar. Nothing to see.

'This is ATC for Shepherd 187. Everything okay up there?

4

Jack Talbot glanced at his mobile phone, then at the rotary on his desk, then back at the mobile. According to his phone it was approaching 10PM, but he checked the clock ticking away on the wall, just in case. Since he'd taken the plunge and opened his own detective agency, he'd realised that half the job was waiting for the phone to ring, what made today different was that he was expecting it. He turned the channel over on the television set perched in the corner of his living room-cum-office. It must have been a slow news day. The news reader looked bored. She should try watching his clock. He tried to rub the tiredness out of his face when, finally, the rotary phone on his desk burst into life.

He snatched up the receiver, cutting the shrill noise to silence.

'Finally,' Jack said.

'Sorry, delays...' the voice replied.

'Well?' Jack asked, 'How long is it going to be?'

'We've hit a deer on the tracks. It'll be another hour they reckon.'

'Okay,' Jack sighed. 'Give us a call when you're near.

After a brief pause, the voice spoke again, 'I can take a taxi if you like...'

'Bollocks to that. I've been waiting up.'

'Thanks, Jack.'

'See you soon, Danny.'

5

Hannah was trying to focus on the magazine ahead, hoping Nic wouldn't invite her to enjoy the view. But she knew it was coming.

'Wow, look at that...'

Nic took in the lights of the town they passed over below. Every now and then Nic's eye was drawn to the cloud illuminated more and more frequently by the flicker of lightning.

Hannah had her head buried in a magazine, 'I'd rather not.'

'Right. Sorry... It was great of Ruth to bring us and pick us up,' she said, quickly changing the subject.

'She's such a worry wart,' Hannah said as the fasten seatbelts sign blinked out.

THE VANISHING OF FLIGHT 187

Nic smiled, finally turning away from the window. 'It's sweet.'

Hannah shrugged; eyes glued to the magazine. 'I suppose. It can get a bit much. It's just since mum...'

'I can imagine.' Nic glanced back at the cloud. It was almost glowing. 'But it's still sweet. I've always liked Ruth.'

They were talking across the vacant middle seat, happy to be sitting away from the half-drunk businessmen at the airport who tried some particularly clumsy flirting. Their original flight had been cancelled and the company had booked the next available, which happened to be a budget, so they'd booked the full row of three seats to give them more space, probably saving money on the original tickets in the process.

The shapely attendant was dragging the drinks trolley along the aisle behind Nic, and Hannah lowered her magazine. She hated flying without a drink. She could have a few if she wanted. They had a free night in Frankfurt before tomorrow morning's meeting.

Ruth had been great since mum died, and they both knew it. It was just sad that she couldn't have a bit more fun. So serious. 'She's alright,' Hannah said sarcastically, Nic catching the meaning.

The fasten seatbelts sign flashed back on with a soft *bong!* over the intercom.

'Fasten seatbelts,' the pilot said in soothing tones. Hannah hadn't bothered removing hers, but she noticed Nic quickly clicking hers back into place.

'Drinks?' The attendant smiled. The smile looked forced. Like she just wanted to get service over with and have a drink herself. Unless the seatbelt sign coming back on meant there was something serious going on...

'Vodka and coke please. With ice.' Hannah replied quickly, as if the offer could be withdrawn at any second. 'Nix?'

Nic's eyes lit up, like she'd been waiting to see what Hannah ordered and just hoped that the request included alcohol. 'The same please.'

The plane shuddered gently, and Hannah gripped the armrests oh-so-slightly harder. She was okay with flying, just as long as that flight was smooth, and she didn't realise they were in mid-air. A gentle shudder she could handle, anything more and that single might have to be a double. The attendant never batted an eye at the momentary shudder. She poured out the drinks and Hannah admired her nail job as she handed them over.

'Cash or card?' she asked, same someone-get-*me*-a-drink smile on her face.

Nix removed her card from her wallet.

'I'll get it.' Hannah thrust her card across to the attendant.

At the moment the card changed hands, the plane dropped.

A loud bang sounded and a few seats back a woman gasped. A baby started to cry. Until then, Hannah had no idea there was a baby on board. She looked straight at the attendant. The drop had probably only been a few feet, although to Hannah it could just as well have been a mile. The attendant smiled again, this time a warm, genuine smile. Hannah's grip released on the armrests and she smiled back. If it's okay with the flight crew, then it's okay with her. If they worried, then it was time to panic.

'Do you want the receipt?' the attendant asked. Hannah nodded and said thanks, the fasten seatbelts sign bonging again as she moved on.

'Any more turbulence and she might have to come back,' Nic said with a smile.

Hannah smiled back, swigging from her plastic glass. It was her turn, it seemed, to give out fake smiles.

6

'Shepherd 187 this is tower, do you read?'

Sean looked back outside but saw only the lights of the town in the distance, the flight by now long gone. His eyes darted back to the radar. A spray of icy droplets fell down his back. In eight and a half years he'd never lost a flight. He'd spoken to guys on internet forums who had. Steve had to take leave for a couple of weeks when he had an incident just after Sean had started. But that was ice. During take-off. Only a few injuries, granted some were serious but still... 187 was already up. Something happened to a flight in mid-air... Maybe he'd need something stronger than beer tonight.

Flight 187's blip appeared on the screen. He started to breathe again.

'This is Shepherd 187...'

The pilot's voice came back calm and he glanced across to a pale looking Steve who'd been listening in on the full exchange. Steve wiped imaginary sweat from his brow.

'Yes, just a little—'

Then the pilot's words were cut off mid-sentence. The tone in his voice sounded normal. Not panicked. Like he was going through the motions. Nothing to worry about.

So why am I shitting myself?

Sean drew in a deep breath. 'This is tower. Do you read, 187? Shepherd one, eight—'

'This is Shepherd 187...'

Now the message was fading in and out with static. And the pilot sounded different. Uncertain.

'Not sure if you c— ...on the radar, but ther— ...unusual—'

The words cut off again. Sean glanced across at Steve, Steve was getting ready to land the flight from Tenerife, but his face was pale, and his eyes had an odd, haunted look... like he was reliving an awful experience. That same cold sweat fell over him and once again he glanced at the radar. He felt sickness rise in his throat and his mind was racing trying to recall protocols from training.

'187, are you there?'

He just stared at the radar, watching it trace the skies, only picking up Steve's flight from Tenerife.

'Er... Steve... I think we might have a problem.'

THE VANISHING OF FLIGHT 187

7

The shrill ring of the telephone shattered the silence in the warm bedroom. Adam Shepherd's eyes fell on the alarm clock and a chill stole over him. For the phone to ring at this hour meant something was horribly wrong. He took a deep breath, reached across for the lamp and tapped the base. Gentle warm light filled the room but the shred of comfort it gave was obliterated when the phone rang again. Only airline employees had that number, and they were told to only use it in an emergency.

'Yes?'

He sat up, no longer tired. This qualified.

'Say that again.'

Sickness rose in him.

'Can't you get hold of them? ... Well what do we pay them for? ... So wake them up like you woke me up!'

He stood and surveyed the room for clothes.

'Have the press got hold of this yet?... Well, we'll see how long that lasts... I'll be there in 20 minutes. I'll meet you at the entrance.'

Adam raced to the airport. They had an office there and he was rushing to meet his senior staff. He'd had time to get dressed and nothing more. He hoped that someone had time to get coffee. The roads were quiet and as he neared the airport, he was relieved to see that the doors weren't surrounded with gangs of reporters and flashing cameras as he'd imagined.

He pulled up to the barrier and touched his security tag

to it. The arm raised and he pulled through and straight into a parking spot. His assistant was waiting, and she'd had time to get coffee. She handed him the coffee, then a note. Inside, he strode along the corridor, his assistant struggling to keep pace. He read the note as he walked, passing it back to his assistant just as they reached the doors. A team of people he hadn't met since their interview four years ago were waiting inside. His assistant skipped through the closing door and Adam turned to face his crisis management team.

8

Outside the station Jack waited, leaning against his car, in the warm night air. A flow of tired passengers trickled from the low, long building, either meeting loved ones or hopping into taxis, just like he had that cold winter's night in York months ago. The trickle was dying off when at last, his friend emerged from the building and scanned his surroundings. Jack stood and waved, and Daniel Cross spotted him. After what had happened in on the North York Moors it came as no small relief for Jack to see him walking without a limp. He reached out a hand and smiled. Daniel Cross mirrored the gesture and shook his hand firmly.

'Thanks for coming to get me.'

'No problem.' He smiled and took his friend's bag. 'I've got to ask,' Jack said, dropping the bag into the back seat, 'was that a *mobile* phone you called me from?' Jack grinned knowing his friend's aversion to modern technology.

'Alright, alright,' Cross smiled at the ribbing. He

produced a flip phone from his pocket. 'I thought biting the bullet and getting one would be easier than listen to your constant abuse.'

'Daniel Cross moving into the 20th century. And how's the leg?'

Cross shrugged a little. A gesture so small he probably didn't know himself he'd done it. 'Not bad. Gives me a bit of gyp when it's damp. But no limp.'

'Still managed to be the last one out,' Jack said, smiling.

'So, how have things been?' Cross asked once they were on their way.

'Not bad. Got myself a flat. Doubles as my office.'

Cross smiled. 'Jack Talbot PI,'

'That's me. Not all it's cracked up to be, but it's an honest living.'

'How so?'

The radio was announcing a breaking news story when Jack turned it off. Cross seemed a little perturbed, a tiny reaction he sensed more than saw. Jack wasn't sure at what it was and pressed on.

'Ah well, you know,' he said, quite sure that Daniel Cross didn't know, or he wouldn't have asked, 'it's mostly doing work on injury claims for businesses. Following blokes on crutches, making sure they aren't on the take. Got a journo friend who chucks a juicy titbit my way every now and then.'

'So it's not all snooping on cheating spouses?' Cross asked with a grin.

'Only when times are hard. More hassle then it's worth, I can tell you. Messy stuff. My camera skills have improved though. How about you?'

The two had spoken since the Breyer case, but only in brief snatches of conversation on the phone or the odd email, nothing in depth, just two friends exchanging pleasantries. Jack wondered if they would have kept in touch if they hadn't almost died.

'Ah you know, plodding along. Still lecturing here and there. Assisting the police. Doing my own investigations.'

Jack remembered a conversation with a detective up in York, Wheeler or something was the name, where Cross mentioned his investigations. Hauntings and UFOs.

'Glad you finally made it down, anyway.'

Daniel Cross never answered, just turned to his window and watched as the town passed by his window.

They pulled up to Jack's apartment block. A tall grim building closer to the wrong part of town than the right. Broken bottles in the gutters and a boarded-up window on a nearby shop covered in graffiti. The front door to Jack's place was unassuming, nothing to suggest it might be where you could hire a private detective, but that's how Jack liked it. To knock on his door, they had to be serious. They traipsed up a single flight of stairs and Jack opened the front door and led Cross into the hallway. Two doors to the right, a door at the end, and a turn to the left.

Jack pointed to the door straight ahead. 'That's the lavvy, bathroom's next door.'

Cross nodded. They turned into the first room. A normal

living room, television in the corner, settee along the wall: the only thing that suggested it was a PI's office was the desk facing the door.

'The settee pulls out into a bed,' said Jack pointing at the sofa. 'Have a seat, I'll get the drinks.'

Cross's face suggested he wasn't sure if that drink would be tea, or something stronger.

'Tea okay?' Jack said, sensing the awkwardness. 'Or something stronger?'

'Have you got anything stronger?'

Jack smiled. 'It's okay. I've got a handle on it now. Stop when I want.'

'I don't want to lead you astray...'

'Daniel, it's fine.'

Cross seemed relieved. 'Don't suppose you've got any Scotch. I've gone off the Wild Turkey lately.'

Jack just smiled again and left the room. He ventured along the corridor and into the kitchen, grabbing two tumblers from the cupboard. As he was dropping the ice cubes into them with a satisfying clunk, a shout came from the living room.

'Mind if I put the telly on?'

'Go for it.'

The last time he saw Cross, he didn't even have a television set of his own. He had zero interest in TV. He forgot about it and carried on preparing the drinks, opening the bottle of Glenfiddich he'd bought the day before.

Cross shouted from the office, 'Jack?'

Jack walked in to see Cross standing in front of the screen.

'Look at this Jack.'

Jack stood beside Cross and absently handed him a tumbler, all the while staring at the breaking news story on the TV.

'That breaking story once again: Shepherd Airlines Flight 187, bound for Frankfurt has vanished from radar.'

Jack stared at the TV. 'That's the local airport.

Cross turned to Jack, 'Should we have a look?'

Jack drained his glass in one go.

9

Adam had managed to stop pacing the meeting room at the airport. He'd rolled his shirt sleeves up and was leaning against the back of one of the chairs, eyeing his crisis management team. The first to speak was a black man he'd put in charge some four years back. Tony. Smartly dressed, he looked calm and relaxed and Adam was wondering how he did it. Then again, chaos was his wheelhouse.

'Sir, it was the 2145 flight to Frankfurt. Flight 187.'

Angela, a bookish woman took over before Adam could speak. 'Radar contact was lost approximately thirteen minutes after take-off.'

'How many on board?' Adam asked.

Tony cleared his throat. 'One hundred and seventy-five souls, sir.'

'Jesus Christ.'

He felt sick.

'We're still receiving data from the tower...'

Tony kept talking but the sounds faded out. The TV in the background played as they waited for the media to catch wind of what was going on. He just hoped that nobody had cut corners anywhere. If they had, lawsuits could end him. Let it be a mistake. Someone else's mistake. Faulty transponders or radar malfunction. Anything.

'Sir.'

Tony was staring at him.

'We need to prepare a statement to give to the press. This won't stay a secret for long.'

Adam straightened his tie, swigged the black coffee that had been awaiting him and swept his silver hair back with his hands. He nodded.

The press getting hold of this was his worst nightmare. Calling into question everything he'd worked so hard to build. This wasn't a massive airline with teams of people designed to control everything. It was him, his media management guy, a lawyer. This could get away from them fast.

'Mr Shepherd?'

Adam looked up to Angela and noticed all eyes were on the television screen. The story had made the news.

10

'Vanished. What does that even mean?' Jack said as they raced to the airport.

Cross shrugged. 'It's odd wording, I'll give you that. Maybe they're trying to be sensitive.'

Jack shook his head. 'If it was a crash, they'd have just said so. Pilot error or bird strike or whatever. But "vanished"? Something's wrong.'

'No, you're right,' was all Cross said.

Jack leaned forward to see past Cross before turning onto the main road and saw that his friend had an odd look about him. He wrote it off as nothing more than the thrill of the chase, after all, had he not seen the same look when they were on the Laszlo Breyer case? No. He had seen that look before, but it wasn't excitement. It was something else. It was some sort of foreknowledge.

'Jesus,' Cross said, voice faint.

Jack looked up at the airport entrance that was coming into view from around the corner.

'Christ. It looks like Black Friday.'

Reporters, photographers, television news crews, all being held back by airport security and police. In amongst the throng, were crowds of civilians, some trying to make flights of their own, some probably family members of those on board. They were forcing their way through, showing ID, passports, driving licences. Jack pulled up in the nearest available space and he and Cross leapt out and headed straight for the chaos.

A police officer held up his hand as they arrived at the doors.

'We've come to pick up a friend,' Jack said without

missing a beat. 'From Majorca.'

'ID,' the officer replied.

Jack showed his driver's licence to the cop, and he let both him and Cross inside. The terminal building was nothing like the madness outside. A strange air circulated, bewildered family members staring at the departures board, where Flight 187 sat amongst the rest of the flights bereft of data. No arrival time, no flight time. Just a lonely name that drew despairing sobs from friends and family below. That in stark contrast to the excited chatter of press and the nervous apprehension apparent in the body language of those about to board their own flights. Their movements robotic like they had stumbled into someone else's dream.

'There's something very creepy about all this,' Cross whispered from behind a hand.

All Jack could do was nod.

The rest of the airport had come to a standstill, shop workers and the staff not required for security and checking-in dotted around, speculating at the bizarre events surrounding Flight 187. Jack peered across the way and saw a familiar face.

He nudged Cross. 'Come on.'

They marched across the marble floor and approached a trio of animated men, doubtlessly speculating at what was unfolding. One of the three turned, saw Jack, and instinctively moved away from the others, his friends carrying on almost as if they hadn't noticed him leave in the excitement.

Jack nodded a hello and then gestured to Cross, 'Damien Spade, this is Daniel Cross.'

Damien was wearing blue jeans and that tatty green jacket he always wore.

'How did you get in?' Damien asked.

'Said I'd come to meet someone.'

'Same,' replied Damien. 'What's that look for?'

'Because you look like a journalist.'

'That obvious, huh?'

Jack turned his back to the wall, standing between Cross and Damien, the confusion before him adding to his own bemusement.

Jack said to Damien, 'What do we know?'

'Not much. Flight took off ten o'clock - late, went missing not long after. Disappeared off radar. Most likely explanation is—'

'Mid-air explosion,' Jack finished. 'Terrorism?'

'You know what these things are like. Nobody's giving too much away. There's just something about this seems...' he scanned the airport, sizing up the chaos, looking like Jack felt, 'I don't know. The way they said "vanished" from radar...'

'That's what we said,' Jack replied.

'I've managed to get hold of the flight manifest. List of passengers.'

'You don't waste any time,' Jack said, genuinely impressed.

'If you're not fast, you're last. I can forward it on if you like. So what are you doing here?' Damien asked.

'Just noseying about really. We were watching the news and...'

THE VANISHING OF FLIGHT 187

'Damo.'

Damien got a tap on the shoulder and he turned away to where his friend was pointing.

Jack's eyes moved in the opposite direction to a door. Unmarked like a service entrance, his eye drawn to it only because it opened. He gently elbowed Cross.

'Well, well. What's this?'

Cross followed Jack's gaze. A man, average height, average build, civilian clothing was making his way from the direction of the door, heading to where the offices and meeting rooms were. Cross saw what Jack was getting at.

'Military?' he asked.

'Bingo,' Jack replied. 'Look at how he walks. How he carries himself.'

'He's not walking, he's marching.'

'The uniform's gone, but that's training in action.'

The man glanced across at them as he passed, close-cropped hair, long face, eyes that sloped ever so slightly down outwardly. Again, nothing out of the ordinary, but Jack couldn't help but think he was a facial scar away from a Bond villain.

They watched him march on before he disappeared around a corner. 'The game, it seems, is afoot.'

11

Adam Shepherd was pacing again. How the hell do you just *lose* a plane? He'd been frowning since he got in here and his head started to ache. The sticky patches under his arms that had darkened his sky-blue shirt were testament to the pressure he was under. There had been the criticism of moving the goalposts to squeeze extra money from his passengers: a change in baggage size here, an online booking fee there; but that was all small fry. A storm in a teacup compared to this – an actual real-life disaster. He knew this day had to come at some point, he just wished it wasn't here now. He turned from the window to see all eyes in the room staring at him.

'Sir?'

It was Tony. Tony was young enough to be his son, he supposed. He had an air of calm that Adam was starting to resent. Even though it was his calm that had stopped this whole thing descending into a shit-show. It wasn't *his* business on the line. His reputation. His life. The difference between a 100% safety record and a 99% safety record was much bigger than the one per cent suggested. Insurance premiums. Share prices. They'd see the difference would be much higher than one lousy percent when trading started tomorrow.

'Mr Shepherd,' Tony said. Cool. Calm. 'Tell me again. How it will sound.'

'That we're doing everything we can. We're getting in touch with family members. The coastguard. We're cooperating with all of the relevant safety bodies... Is "bodies" the right word?' he said, but the words echoed like they'd fallen down a well. The word – bodies – it conjured an image of corpses bobbing up and down with white plane fragments in black water. He felt sick.

'We can change the wording, but we have to give them something, all they'll start speculating, and that is the last thing we need. Get in front of this now and we control the narrative.'

The bookish woman nodded. 'If we throw them a bone now, it will stop them from doing too much digging. Buy us time.'

'She's right.' Tony said. 'But it has to happen soon.'

'Do we say it's terrorism?' Adam asked, grasping at whatever he could in the hope of pinning the blame on anyone but his airline.

'No. Nothing like that. We keep it simple until we know more ourselves. This one statement for now. Tell them they will get more when we get more. No questions. Keep it brief. Keep it factual.'

Adam dabbed the sweat from his brow with a damp handkerchief. Through the window he saw a plane soaring into the night. Someone else's plane. If something happened to this one...

For God's sake Adam, what are you saying? Get a grip man. Tony's right.

Before he could turn and nod, he heard a sound that made him jump. One of the conference telephones was ringing. He turned and the woman was listening to whoever had called. He wasn't sure who knew they were even in here.

She locked eyes with Adam before covering the mouthpiece with a hand. 'It's for you.'

'Who is it?' he mouthed.

His question was met with a shrug. Was it terrorists?

Was this their leader claiming responsibility? Or maybe this was the hijackers, calling with demands. With a trembling hand he took the phone and drew a breath to compose himself.

'Adam Shepherd speaking, who's this?'

Once again, all eyes in the room were on him, and this time he turned away from them. Now he hoped they wouldn't see the colour draining from his face.

12

It was about forty minutes later, just as Jack and Cross were about to leave, that an announcement was made. There was to be a press conference and an official statement from the airline. Damien led them through the airport, past grieving families and the cryptic departures board, around the deserted alcohol and perfume shops and into a corridor. Around the corner all the journalists and cameramen from the outside pushed into a media room. The double doors guarded by security men at each side. It was one of these men who stopped Damien.

'Press pass.'

Damien flashed a badge and the security man nodded him inside.

Jack was face to face with this latest hurdle. 'I've left mine in the car.'

'You'll have to go and get it.'

'He's with me,' Damien shouted from inside.

THE VANISHING OF FLIGHT 187

'Where's his camera?' The security guy asked, without looking at him.

Damien shrugged. 'I'll meet you outside.'

Jack and Cross turned away, trudging for the car park. The storm had moved away or fizzled out, but the ground was dry. Hard to believe after what they'd seen inside, but the storm had passed them by. Half an hour later, Damien met up with them in the still of the night.

'Well?' Jack asked.

'You're not going to like it...'

Jack shook his head as they drove home in silence. The radio was still turned off. He hadn't wanted to hear the same story over and over, but as they sat at the latest set of lights, the silence was getting to him.

'Fuck all.'

Jack wasn't really surprised. The airline was hardly going to come out and say it was blown out of the sky if it wasn't, and they had their own internal investigations to do. All it proved was that as far as the airline were concerned, it wasn't something obvious. No explosion; no pilot error; they couldn't confirm a crash, at least, not without wreckage.

'Well, they obviously don't have anything to tell. Nothing they'd be happy to share at this time anyway. It does leave the relatives hanging though.'

'Oh well,' Jack said, 'It doesn't really matter to us. We'll be stuck watching the news for developments like everybody else.'

'Morbid curiosity,' Cross said, absently.

'Hmm?'

'We were just going for our own morbid curiosity, I said.'

'Right. I'm wide awake now though. Too much excitement at bedtime.'

Cross just nodded.

Back at the flat, they had fresh drinks. The news loop was repeating the little information their airport trip had already revealed. Shepherd was finishing his press conference as they turned the telly on. He looked tired and pressured, shadows under his eyes, sweat on his brow, Jack was sure he'd have patches under his arms under that suit Jacket. Cross had barely said a word since the airport. His silence perhaps brought about by the lack of finality from their airport excursion. He felt a little of it himself, God alone knew what this limbo must have been like for the poor families.

'He seems like a nice chap.' Cross said, finally breaking the silence.

'The airline owner?'

'Damien.'

'Yeah he's alright. I had to threaten a guy with going to the press to get him to pay his business partner money he owed. He thought I was bluffing. So I met Damien.'

'Is that ethical?'

'We're in the trenches here, old boy. "All's fair" and all that.'

Cross's eyes brightened; that yearning for excitement that dragged him into the case of Laszlo Breyer shining through.

'Anyway,' Jack continued, 'every now and then, he'll

throw a bit of business my way if he's at a dead end.'

Cross seemed impressed. 'An investigative journalist.'

Jack nodded as he drank, emptying his glass. 'Bloody good one too. A young guy but he's old school. Says he wants to make the establishment sweat, like Julian Assange, with a folder of secrets he'll release if anything happens to him—'

'Dead man's switch,' Cross interrupted.

'Right. Anyway, he always agrees to share whatever he's got with me, after I chucked that story his way. Actually, he was telling me about this weird—'

Jack stopped dead when Adam Shepherd came back on the television.

'What?' Cross asked.

They hadn't paid much attention the first time around, only catching the tail end of the presser, but now it was on from scratch.

'There!' Jack said, grabbing the remote.

He rewound the conference back to the start and let it play from the beginning.

'Watch. Here.' Jack pointed to the right of the screen.

Cross waited as Adam Shepherd told Damien and the other members of the assembled press that they were doing everything they could and cooperating with anyone and everyone.

'There!' Jack shouted again, freezing the action.

'Well, well,' Cross said. 'Is that...'

It was. Just leaning into the shot. Only half of his face was visible, but those gently sloping narrow eyes. The long, thin face.

They both said at once. 'The military man.'

Jack let the conference play on.

'It's definitely him.'

'One hundred per cent,' Cross agreed, 'but what's this got to do with the military? MI5?'

Jack had no idea. All he knew for sure was that tonight, he'd get little in the way of sleep.

CHAPTER TWO

JACK STUMBLED BACK and forth from the fridge, yawning as he prepared scrambled eggs. He'd turned the radio on first thing, but then turned it down. The chat between classic songs of the sixties was dominated by the missing flight and Jack wondered if they'd been given a list of songs not to play. No *Back in the USSR*. No John Denver. And Jefferson Airplane? Forget it. Much to Jack's disappointment, while he'd been in that restless sleep, there had been nothing in the way of new developments. The kettle rumbled and clicked, and he poured two coffees. Before he could shout Cross, he shuffled into the kitchen.

'Morning.'

Cross was usually all rise-and-shine but today looked like he'd done little in the way of sleeping himself.

'Eggs. Coffee.'

Cross sat himself at the kitchen table. Jack slid a plate before him and sat opposite with his own.

'Any developments?' Cross gestured towards the radio with his fork.

Jack shook his head. 'Same old shit from last night. 24-hour news cycle. On a loop waiting for something to break.'

Cross shrugged a little, tucking into his breakfast. When he'd finished the first mouthful he asked. 'What's on the agenda for today then?'

He'd cleared his schedule knowing that Cross was coming to visit but had nothing planned for his time here. He thought he'd see what Cross was interested in and take it from there. Jack swallowed the mouthful of egg and replied, 'Not sure really. I'm not on a case, so whatever you want.'

'I've brought my sketchbook. There's an old abbey not too far from here.'

History was never a topic that enthralled Jack. If he couldn't use the information right now, it was no use to him. Whatever was left of the crumbling abbey was a forty-minute drive away, but the sky was blue, so the drive out would be a good one. There was a pencil drawing at the top of the stairs in Cross's house. A drawing of his son.

'Wait a minute. That picture of Nathan at your place. You did that?'

Cross smiled. 'That's me.'

'A man of many talents... Lucy Breyer painted you know.'

Cross nodded. 'She's good. She has a good eye.'

Jack cleared his throat. He'd promised Cross he'd tell him about what happened to Lucy Breyer one day, but today was not that day. He quickly moved on.

'Before we go, I want to give Damien a ring. Tell him about our friend at the press conference.'

'Right. Any thoughts there?'

'Not too sure.' Jack swigged his coffee. 'The only reason I can imagine MI5 getting involved is if there was a hijacking. That, or terrorism.'

'Is that who you reckon he is? MI5?'

THE VANISHING OF FLIGHT 187

'After laying awake thinking about it most of the night, that's the best I could come up with.' Jack looked across at his friend, 'Why, have you got another theory?'

Cross shrugged. 'A couple of ideas. More along the lines of the non-conventional.'

'I'd expect nothing less,' Jack said with a grin.

Cross ignored the ribbing and continued. 'The things you mentioned are the most likely answers.'

Jack rose from the table and dumped his dishes into the sink. Cross carried on.

'Of course, there have been cases in the past of flights going missing. Emelia Erhart, The Bermuda Triangle, even cases where UFOs were spotted on radar...'

Jack nodded, more to humour his friend, 'It's far too early in the morning for me to be getting into discussions about the Bermuda Triangle.'

'Well...' Cross finished the last mouthful of food and continued, 'More than likely it's what you said, but we shouldn't rule anything out.'

This was a good time to draw a line under it and move along. 'We'll see what develops,' he said. 'Right. I'll jump in the shower, then we can get ready, and get going.'

While Cross was humming tunelessly in the shower, Jack dressed, dropped onto the bed and called Damien.

'I'm 99% sure. When someone's been in the military, it's hard to unlearn that sort of thing. You carry yourself in a certain way.'

'And he was at the presser?' Damien asked.

'When you watch it, he leans into shot for half a second, but it's him.'

'Hhm...' Damien paused, processing this new information. 'The thick plottens.' That was what he always said whenever something got interesting. 'Probably terrorists then,' he added.

Jack replied, 'Or a hijacking.'

Damien *hhhm'd* again. 'Weird that they haven't just come out and said that though - if that's what it was.'

'Right,' Jack agreed. 'Anything new from your side?'

'Cock all. But I'll keep you posted.'

Jack was about to end the call when he remembered something. 'Did you send over that passenger list?'

'Shit, not yet. I'll do it after breakfast.'

'Thanks.' Jack wanted to ask where he got it from so quickly but didn't want to hear Damien's spiel about revealing sources.

They ended the call and after a few minutes, Cross emerged from the office ready to go.

'All set?'

Cross lifted his leather carry all which Jack could only presume held a sketchpad and pencils and nodded.

'I put the bed away. The bedding just goes behind, right?'

'Yeah. You didn't have to; I'd have seen to it.'

Jack reached for the front door, and just as he grabbed the handle, there was a knock.

2

Jack and Cross stopped dead and exchanged a glance. Jack had no cases open and his phone hadn't rung all morning. There was another knock. Jack leaned towards the spyhole. At the other side of the door was a woman with dark, shoulder length hair. Jack thought he caught a glimpse of fear in the brief knotting of her eyebrows. She knocked again.

'Is the room tidy?' Jack whispered to Cross.

Cross nodded. Cross's own house had been spotless when Jack was there before, so that nod was enough.

'Shall I go to the kitchen?'

Jack thought for a moment and smiled. Without answering he opened the door.

'Good morning.'

The woman lowered her hand. Jack had caught her pre-knock. She was smartly dressed *not short of money* medium height, slim but athletic *not physical work, the suit suggests an office, but takes care of herself, goes jogging, and the job probably comes with a gym membership.*

'Jack Talbot?' she said.

Jack and Cross both took a step back.

'Please. Come in.' Jack held the door open and gestured for her to step into his office. Cross followed Jack into the room and sat on the settee in the corner as Jack took his place at his desk across from the woman. She was mid-thirties, attractive but serious looking and not wearing any rings.

Married to the job?

Jack turned his own wedding ring on his finger for a

second. 'I'm Jack Talbot, and this,' he gestured at Cross, 'is my colleague Daniel Cross.'

'Ruth Draper,' she said nodding a hello at Jack, ignoring Cross completely.

Not rudeness. Urgency. Concern.

'How did you find me?'

'You came highly recommended by a friend. You worked on an injury claim for him.'

Jack's mind searched for the connection. An injury claim he worked on for a male client who looked like the sort of person Ruth Draper might mingle with.

Geoff Robbins. Had an employee make an injury claim.

One of Geoff's employees claimed he could barely walk after a fall at work, but Jack photographed him playing football with his son in the back yard of his house. No crutches in sight. Must have saved Ted a small fortune. Paid well. Ted was well off, therefore...

This might be a payday.

'Can I offer you a drink?' Jack asked out of nothing more than politeness, knowing that the answer would return in the negative.

'No. Thanks.'

Jack flipped to a clean page of his A4 pad and grabbed his pencil. 'How can I help?'

'My sister is missing.'

Missing persons cases were tough. If there was no sign of a struggle the police wouldn't really get too involved. If someone didn't want to be found, then finding them was trickier than most would imagine. Though that just kept the meter running on Jack's tab, and Ruth Draper looked like she could afford it.

Ruth continued. 'If you've been watching the news, you'll have seen that there's been a plane... A flight has gone missing. On the way to Frankfurt.'

Jack stopped writing and looked up. In the corner of his eye he saw Cross lean forward in his seat.

'Yes, it's been all over the news.'

'Basically, Mr Talbot, my sister is on that flight. My sister and her friend.'

Is *on that flight. Not was. She's holding on to the belief her sister is alive.*

There was a pause while Ruth composed herself, and Jack instinctively pushed the box of tissues closer to his potential new client. Jack wondered what he was supposed to do for this woman. This wasn't a missing persons case; Ruth's sister was somewhere in the English Channel. He took advantage of the pause to speak.

'Coming back to your... case. Your sister—'

'Hannah.'

Jack scribbled the name on the pad. 'Hannah and her friend are on a missing plane... That's not what I... I suppose what I'm trying to ask is what exactly it is that you'd like me to do.'

'Have you seen the press conference? The one delivered by the airline owner?'

Jack nodded, 'Adam Shepherd.'

'He's hiding something.'

Jack glanced over at Cross and his mind (probably

Cross's too) went to the military man.

'Hiding what exactly?'

'That's what I want you to find out.'

'Ms Draper—'

'Ruth.'

'Ruth, I'm not really sure I can help. Why do you want this information?'

Ruth shuffled in her seat. 'I think the airline could be at fault. I work as a lawyer—'

'So you plan to sue.'

'If I can get proof, absolutely.'

A pregnant silence hung in the air.

'All due respect, that kind of thing could take time, and if I may be blunt, it would not come cheap.'

'Money is no object. I'd pay a week at a time. Plus expenses. If you get me what I'm looking for before the week is up, you keep the difference.'

Jack could only look at Ruth Draper. There was a desperation in her eyes that made him uncomfortable.

'Again, Ruth, forgive me for being blunt, but none of this will bring Hannah back.'

There was a silence and now Ruth Draper snatched a tissue from the box. She gently pressed the tissue against the tear that had run down her face.

'The airline is lying. Find proof. That's all I ask.'

Her eyes stared at Jack. Jack tapped his pencil off the notepad while he weighed things up. He glanced again at Cross sitting out of her line of sight. He shrugged as if to say, "why not?"

Jack looked back at Ruth Draper.

'What was the name of your sister's friend?'

3

Jack and Ruth stood at the doorway to his flat and she handed him a business card.

'If you do decide to take my case, I shall expect regular updates.'

Jack nodded. 'I'll be in touch by the end of the day.'

He saw Ruth out and darted back into the living room.

'Let's go.'

Cross was standing, gazing out of the window. He snatched his car keys from his desk. Cross turned, confused.

'Chop chop.'

'Where to?'

Cross ambled towards him and Jack grabbed his arm, marching him from the flat.

'Follow the white rabbit.' Jack grinned.

They were heading from Jack's place in the industrial part of town in the general direction of the nicer neighbourhoods. Which was a start. A good start. Ruth's car sat at the red light, a few cars down from Jack's. Jack had grown tired of working out of his flat. He dreamed of an office with his name stencilled on the door. For that, he needed a cash injection. This case of Hannah Draper could be it.

'Where are we going exactly?' Cross asked.

'Wherever the lovely Ruth Draper is leading us.'

Cross replied to Jack's glance with another confused look.

'Due diligence, Danny boy. If I'm taking this case, I need to know that Ruth Draper is not some nutter dressed as money to waste old Jack Talbot's time.'

'That happens?'

The light turned green, and they pulled away, following Ruth.

'You wouldn't believe.'

They drove for a short while until eventually, the cars between them had turned away, Jack dropping back to compensate for the lack of cover. By the time they stopped they were in the part of town Jack had only heard of - smooth roads, green lawns, detached houses. Ruth pulled into a long driveway and got out, heading straight inside.

'Nice place.'

'She's got the money all right,' Jack replied. 'I wouldn't take this case normally.'

'How come?' Cross frowned.

'It's hard to get a win. Chances are we'll—'

'*We?*'

Jack carried on like the interruption never happened. '...scratch around for a couple of days, find absolutely nothing, and then some poor bastard in Holland'll find a seat washed up on a beach. Ruth's holding on to the idea that her sister is still alive. That plane turns up in bits and Ruth's giving this case the hot potato treatment.'

'If you look at it that way then it's an easy payday...'

Jack shook his head. 'Not ideal. Looks like a fail. Here's a client, well off, a recommendation from someone else, also loaded, who'll probably tell her friends that she hired a private detective and he was useless. Don't use Jack Talbot.'

Cross shrugged, 'If you feel like that, don't take the case.'

'Need the money. As much as I like my flat, I'd like to have a real office, instead of a desk in a living room.'

'Okay...' Cross started. 'Well it looks like she's got the money...' he tailed off.

'Thing is, I won't know until I get the passenger list off Damien whether Hannah really was on that flight, and all we got for the friend was a first name...' he paused letting Cross fill the blank.'

'Nicola.'

'Nicola...'

'Lewis or Luton or something—'

'Which is odd.'

'What?'

'Well, 2019 and Ruth doesn't know the last name of her sister's friend. You know, social media and all...'

Cross paused a minute. 'I don't use social media. Ruth does look the serious type. Maybe she hasn't got time for that sort of thing.'

Jack smiled at Cross. 'Now you're thinking.'

Jack looked back at the house. He'd seen a shape pass by one of the upstairs windows a few minutes ago, but nothing since. Ruth Draper looked like a woman who'd slept little the night before. Jack's money was on her going straight to bed.

'What happens now?'

Jack glanced at his watch. 'We know that they work together, and where they work, let's try to get a last name for Nicola.'

Jack sent another message to Damien, asking for the passenger list ASAP before firing up the car and setting off for home.

4

Back in Jack's office, Cross was surfing the news reports for an update, Jack tapping away at the computer. He was checking social media, trying to get a surname for Hannah's friend. He was also aware that he was wasting time. The more time he spent not proving Adam Shepherd and the airline were hiding something, the more chance the plane would turn up. Even if it was just bits of it. Those shreds of fuselage or burnt luggage would likely end Ruth's interest, effectively ending the case before he'd even taken it, which meant doing anything was time wasting.

Would the end of Ruth's interest end his own? There was something about all of this he didn't like. Ruth's vague details. Could it really be that she was too wrapped up in her own affairs to know the last name of her sister's best friend? And then there was the flight. Trying to find info on a plane, when the whole news media and anyone with anything to do with flight safety was using their much greater resources to do the same seemed ridiculous. But it was more than that; there was one thing above all else he found disconcerting - the military man. He gave Jack the creeps, more even than Laszlo Breyer had.

'I'm trying to get a last name for the friend.'

'To what end?' Cross replied.

'Hmm?'

'Why do you want to know the last name?'

'Curiosity mainly.'

Cross looked away from the news at Jack. 'There's something weird, isn't there?'

Jack was relieved to hear someone else voice the concerns. He recalled Daniel Cross's peculiar ability to sense what he was thinking and made a mental note to ask what trickery he was using when there were less pressing matters at hand.

'Thank Christ. I thought it was just me.'

Cross shook his head. A quick, brief gesture. 'No, no. You're right to be doubtful. Something very odd is going on. I think Ruth is onto something there.'

'I just want to be sure that it isn't Ruth that's giving me the vibe, that's all.'

'I don't think it is,' Cross said, not shifting his gaze from the news, 'but you're right to check.'

Jack tapped the keys on his computer. 'Well, all of Hannah's social media accounts are locked. Ruth's influence I imagine. And it's Saturday, so I doubt there's anyone at their office, but with what's going on, maybe there'll be someone in. It's worth a try.'

He found the number for Hannah's office on their website. It was a hotel booking site and the moment the page opened a window popped up asking if he needed help. Hannah and Nicola's project - and the reason for their trip to Frankfurt in the first place. He shuddered.

He dialled the number and while the call was connecting, ripped a blank sheet of paper from the pad and rolled it into a ball.

'What on earth are you—'

Jack shushed Cross and placed the receiver on the edge of his desk and pushed a button on the phone. The ringing burst from the speaker. After a few rings, Jack was surprised when someone answered. The moment they did, he held the ball of paper next to the phone and started scrunching it.

'Hello?' Jack shouted. 'Can you hear me okay? This line is awful.'

'Yes I can hear you,' the other voice said, slightly raised, but coming through with crystal clarity. 'Just about.'

The ball crinkled in Jack's hand the whole time and he spoke over it. 'I've got an urgent message, but Nic isn't answering her phone and I seem to have lost her email. I was wondering...'

'Who, sorry?'

'Nico— Lew—' Jack let his voice die away as if the bad signal had taken it.

'Nic?'

He raised his voice, 'Her name is Nicola L—'

'Nicola Lutton?'

'That's right, Nicola Lutton.'

Cross grinned with childlike enthusiasm.

'I'm sorry, I'm afraid—' Jack spoke louder again. 'Let me

call you back, I can't cope with this line.'

He put the phone down and dropped the crushed paper to his desk. Nicola Lutton. He typed it into social media and got a hit on the first website.

'Nicola Lutton. Works at EasyAccommodation.com; Correct. Friends with... Hannah Draper. Photos... unlocked.'

Cross left the TV playing and stood beside Jack at the desk.

Jack looked at the picture of Nicola with her long flowing locks of strawberry blonde hair and bright eyes. 'Good looking girl. Always a bonus.'

'That's not very professional, Jack.'

Jack stopped what he was doing and turned to look at Cross. 'Which means, Daniel, that she takes lots of photos... Selfies... Clues.'

Cross's cheeks reddened. 'Oh.'

'Oh.' Jack said, turning back to the computer, smiling to himself.

They were scanning a folder of photos named "Birthday BBQ", looking for anything that might say where Nicola lived.

'If we're lucky, there'll be a photo with a street sign.'

'You are kidding,' Cross was shocked.

'You'd be surprised,' Jack said. 'Failing that, anything that might hint at where they are.'

They scanned through the pictures, Cross noting, 'Looks a bit like Ruth's neighbourhood.'

'It's certainly fancy...'

Then there was a group photo.

'Bingo.'

Cross was confused. 'Bingo?'

Jack turned to Cross. 'Tell me what you see. Be specific.'

Cross took on a more serious look, one that said, "challenge accepted".

'Let's see. Okay, we've got a group of young people.'

'More specific.'

Cross paused. 'Eleven young people... in a nicely maintained garden.'

'Better. Keep going.'

'There are tall trees in the background. Conifers?'

'Good.'

'And in the distance... The middle distance,' he corrected, 'a water tower behind the trees.'

'Very good. And in the bottom corner of the shot? Something that will no doubt be in loads of the other pictures...'

'A swimming pool.'

'Specific.'

'The corner of a swimming pool?'

'Jackpot.'

Jack loaded up a map on the laptop. 'So I'm looking for...'

'A property in a nice neighbourhood, likely not too far from Ruth Draper's, tree lined, near a water tower, with a rectangular pool.'

'Why rectangular?'

'Law of averages. Who has a square pool?'

'Impressive, Dr Cross,' Jack said, scouring the images

online.

'How do we know these pictures were taken at her place?'

'I'd imagine it's her parents place, unless she's ridiculously rich. To answer your question, the weather in the pictures is good, which hints at the time of year. It's her birthday, which according to her page is in July. Is it possible a friend with a pool has invited her around to their place? Of course. We just have to hope we're lucky.'

'All of this is time we could be looking for clues that the airline is lying.'

'You're absolutely right,' Jack said. 'I just want to be sure that Ruth Draper isn't first.

5

Jack pulled up just along from the house he'd found online and opened one of the cheese and pickle sandwiches he'd made for lunch. Like Ruth's neighbourhood, the area was neat lawns, tall gates and detached houses; quiet and peaceful, a big change from the traffic and noise they'd just left behind.

'Look,' Cross said. 'That's it.'

'You need a bit of luck.'

Jack knew they'd just got a huge slice of it. The house they suspected of being Nic Lutton's had a driveway packed with cars. Family members and friends coming to offer support. This is where mum and dad Lutton lived.

'It looks like everything Ruth said checks out,' Cross said. 'So...'

Jack's phone buzzed. Jack grabbed his phone from his pocket and started scrolling. Cross was casing the house, eyes darting for movement inside.

'Bingo.' Jack grinned.

'What's that?'

He showed his phone to Cross.

'Email from Damien with the passenger list. I draw your attention to seat 32 F.'

Cross squinted. 'Hannah Draper.'

'And ladies and gentlemen, who do we find in seat 32 D?

'Nicola Lutton.' Cross smiled, enjoying detective work immensely. 'Does that mean you've got a case?'

Jack looked at the house. 'It looks like I've got a case.'

He grabbed his mobile phone and called Ruth. 'Hello? I've decided I'll take the case. I'll email you with bank details and I'll forward any receipts for expenses. You'll get updates every two days with important information. If you want or need anything, or you think of anything that might be important, let me know straight away.'

Jack ended the call and turned to Daniel Cross with a smile. 'Fancy a trip to the airport?'

6

'This seems like an unnecessary expense,' Cross said, inspecting the freshly printed boarding pass.

Jack lifted his passport. 'Props, old boy. If someone asks why I'm at the airport and I can't produce these, it draws attention. These will at least give me an excuse for being there. Plus, I'll need access. They get me it.'

Cross nodded, then frowned. 'What's my excuse?'

'What?'

'What's my story? I haven't got a boarding card. No props.'

'Oh, er...' Jack paused, 'you're just coming to wave me off.'

'Wave you off?'

Jack shrugged, 'You know, "Thanks for coming," and, "Have a safe flight." All that shit.'

'All that shit?'

Cross wasn't quite on the same page.

'It'll be fine. I'm flying, you're waving me off.'

They parked up and entered the terminal. The mood at the airport today was more business as usual – but the events of last night still lingered. The conversations on staff breaks and in shops would be dominated by Flight 187. The strange air was amplified now the place wasn't jammed with reporters. Not that it took much filling. A small airport that made international flights, just one main building and a couple of runways, but they were busy. They were certainly getting their money's worth from the small set-up.

Jack strolled past the arrivals and a disparate group of people who no doubt would be relieved to see whoever they were waiting for, especially after last night. He peered up at the departures board.

'There's yours,' Cross said, 'Malaga. Gate ten.'

'That's not what I'm looking for... There. Amsterdam.

Gate four.'

Cross nodded. 'Shepherd Airlines.'

'You've got it. I'll have to go through security.' He thrust a ten-pound note at Cross. 'Go and buy yourself a magazine and wait in the car. I might be a while. Keep your phone handy, I'll text you.'

Cross nodded and started for the newsagent.

'And get a receipt.'

Cross waved without looking back.

Jack's plan was simple: get as close as he could to the Shepherd Airlines flight crew and see if there was anything he could glean from them about the missing flight. The chances of getting a smoking gun would be slim, but he'd at least be able to get a read on how they reacted.

Once through passport control and the shoes off, belt off, jacket off, rigmarole of security, he milled about the departures lounge, waiting for a sight of the mint green uniforms of Shepherd Airlines. He perused the aisles of duty free until he found what he was looking for. A boxed bottle. It was vodka. He hated vodka. Perfect. He paid for it, collected the receipt, and went to get a coffee. He chose a table outside and sat facing the duty-free shop and the security check he'd just come through. That was where the flight crew for Amsterdam would appear. He hoped.

He fired off a text message to Cross.

'Waiting for flight crew. No sign. Of any, not just Shepherd. Wondering if they come in a different way...'

Jack glanced at his watch. It was already after three. As much as he hated waiting, time flew by too quickly when he was working. He expected Ruth to drop this case as soon as wreckage was found, but now he was in. The question had gripped him. Ruth was right, something was going on here and now he had to know exactly what is was.

Just then, a handsome pilot appeared, followed by his co-pilot and five attendants in dark green. A Shepherd Airlines crew.

He sent a new message.

'Okay. Go time.'

He put the phone away and picked his mark. It would have to be one of the two crew members at the back, rapt in conversation. The tall, tanned, blond guy or the sweet-faced woman, slim, but with an arse that would struggle down the aisle with the drinks trolley. As the pilots passed, Jack made his move.

Head down, he wandered for the back of the line. On contact with the ample-arsed attendant, he dropped the vodka, throwing his passport and boarding card the other direction. The bottle hit the floor and smashed, held in place by the box.

'Jesus!'

'I am so sorry,' the lady said.

Jack stooped to pick up his passport. 'No, it's fine. You know what? It's my fault.'

The guy went for the boarding card.

'I'm just really nervous,' Jack said. 'Especially after last night. What with the crash and everything...'

'It wasn't a crash,' she said.

No doubt. Not vague. One hundred per cent certain.

Jack's throat tightened. The tall guy returned Jack's boarding pass and Jack nodded thanks. But his mind and his focus were all on the woman.

'What do you mean "wasn't a crash"?'

Her cheeks flushed red and the man replied instead.

'We have to go, sir. Enjoy your flight.' He turned to his colleague, 'Come on Kay.'

They exchanged smiles and life in the airport around them continued now that the show was over. But Jack had already felt a shift inside him, only four words *It wasn't a crash* but things had changed. Ruth Draper had been right to be sceptical. Perhaps her sister was alive.

The next step in Jack's plan was in play. He returned to his seat outside the coffee shop and waited.

7

It was only a few minutes before he came along. A cheerful young man, with a shiny bald head and neat, black goatee beard. There was a Hispanic look about him, though Jack couldn't be sure, and all things told, didn't care. It made no difference. He watched as the cleaner pushed the cart to the limp box of broken vodka bottle and carefully swept it onto a dustpan, dispensing it in the black bag. The cleaner mopped up the vodka, dropped a yellow sign to warn others of the wet floor, and went back the way he'd come.

Jack followed.

He called Cross.

'Well?' Cross asked.

THE VANISHING OF FLIGHT 187

'Well something's going on, that's for sure. Listen...' Jack stopped and turned as the cleaner paused to sweep a receipt into his dustpan.

'...I need you to call me back. In ten minutes.'

'Will do.'

He traipsed along, keeping a few yards between himself and the cleaner, following past lines of people waiting to board their flight to Amsterdam (mostly young men, and a couple of hen parties - all already drunk) and neared an unmarked door. This was as close to alone as they were going to get. Just before he disappeared inside, Jack made his move.

'Hi,' Jack said with a smile. 'I was wondering if you could help me.'

'Sure.' The guy smiled back.

Jack held out a hand for the guy to shake, 'My name's Tom, I'm just coming to check the place out, I start work here on Monday.'

The man smiled and shook his hand, 'I'm George.'

'It looks like a cool place to work, I just wanted to make sure I'd made the right decision.'

'Yeah, it's pretty cool. Everybody is pretty friendly and says 'hi' to everyone. You on the cleaning crew?'

'Security.'

He nodded. 'Cool.'

'One thing though, George, I had to park all the way at the back with all of the other cars.'

'No, no,' George said, 'that's just for passengers, if you keep going right to the front and the left, there's a separate part where we all park. It's reserved for employees.'

'Right. That's the one thing I forgot to ask. Thanks a lot, George.'

'No problem, Tom.' He smiled again and shook Jack's hand. 'See you Monday.'

Jack headed back for the security check and right on cue, Cross called. Jack answered.

'Stay on the phone,' he whispered.

He re-entered the security area. A security guard stepped towards him, but before he could tell Jack going out this way was off limits, Jack said, 'Which hospital is she in?'

8

Jack was back in the car. He'd been led through another exit by a sympathetic security team member and was now parked as close as he could get himself to the employees parking. They'd had their eyes glued to that exit long enough for twilight to loom. The airport floodlights flickered on as they waited for the next stage of Jack's plan.

'There wasn't a crash?' Cross said again after a long pause. 'I can't get my head around it.'

'Those were her exact words. Like I said, the guy moved her along pretty sharpish after that. Like they've been told to keep quiet.'

'Let's go over it again.'

It was the third time but still, maybe this time they'd shake something loose.

'Okay,' Jack started. 'No crash means no bomb. So no terrorism.'

'And therefore we can rule out a crash.'

'Right. No accident, no pilot error... The one thing I keep coming back to is that military guy.'

'Military intelligence?'

'I'd say so. Which means we're probably looking at a hijacking.'

Cross frowned. 'That makes no sense though. Whenever there's a hijacking, it's all over the news. Why the secrecy? What's different this time?'

Jack grabbed his phone and pulled up the passenger list. He scrolled through it.

'Secrecy. Sensitive.'

'An international incident? An important passenger?'

'A high-value target.'

'On a budget airline?'

'The last place you'd look...'

Jack scanned for foreign names or a surname he recognised. He saw nothing that jumped out and handed the list to Cross.

'Have a look through that, see if you recognise any names, apart from Hannah and her friend.'

Cross started scrolling, 'What do you make of Adam Shepherd?'

'The airline owner?' Jack shrugged. 'He seems on the level. He just looked tired and under pressure to me. Do you remember back in the early 2000s, there was a fuel strike?'

'Vaguely.'

Of course. Daniel Cross wasn't one for keeping up with

the news.

'It was the first major crisis Tony Blair had as PM.'

'Okay,' Cross said, like a tiny bell was ringing somewhere in his mind.

'Up until that point, Blair had had things pretty easy. The press seemed to love him; he'd never had a real emergency, he always had that fresh, bright eyes look about him...'

'Right.' Cross sounded more definite now.

'He came out the day after it started and gave a presser. He looked haggard. Like he'd barely slept. That's what Adam Shepherd looked like.'

Cross handed the phone back. 'None of the names jump out, but we should have a deeper look online. I've got a theory.'

'And have a look into Mr Shepherd. Just in case.'

Jack pointed at the terminal building and fired the car up.

'Here we go.'

A thickset man left the exit they'd led Jack through and strode towards the employee's car park. Jack vaguely recognised him from inside but couldn't place him. His hair looked as black as pitch in the darkness and went with his uniform. *Probably security.* He squeezed into his car and drove away. Jack Talbot and Daniel Cross followed.

Night had fallen by the time they pulled up on the airport employee's street. It was a little closer to Jack's part of town, cars lining the street rather than parked off road like in Ruth Draper's neighbourhood.

The guy left his car and entered his house without a care.

'What house number was that?'

'Thirty-six.' Cross replied.

Jack started the car again.

'That's it?'

'It's too late now, he might not answer the door at this time. We'll come back first thing.'

They went back to Jack's place and straight to their separate quarters. Tomorrow was going to be a busy day.

9

Jack Talbot and Daniel Cross were sitting where they'd parked the night before. The day was grey and the car was filled with the smell of coffee and bacon sandwiches they'd bought from a local cafe en route. Whoever the guy from the airport they'd followed home the previous night was, he was still at home. Or at least his car was.

'A lot of this job is waiting, isn't it?' Daniel Cross said after he finished the last bite of his sandwich.

Jack never took his eyes off the house. 'You've got no idea. Waiting for someone to come out of somewhere. Or go in. Waiting for a lead. Waiting for info to arrive from a source. That's if you're working. If you haven't got a case, it's worse. Then you're waiting for the phone to ring.'

Now they were waiting for this house to show signs of life. They didn't want to wake him up (nobody likes that) but they wanted to speak to him before he left his house. It was a Sunday, so the chances were it was his day off.

'One thing I never asked you...' Jack said.

'Go on.'

Jack paused briefly. 'How did you get into all this?'

'By "all this", I trust you mean the paranormal.'

'Right.'

'I get asked that a lot.'

It was something Jack had wanted to ask for a long while, but the timing never seemed right. Now it was perfect. 'It's just that...'

Cross waited for Jack to unpack the thoughts he was having, rather than interrupt.

Jack finally went on, '...you seem... well, normal.'

Cross chuckled. 'I get that a lot too. When people hear what I do they expect me to be clad top to toe in black leather like one of those chaps on The Matrix.'

'You've seen The Matrix?'

'I've seen the posters.'

'Oh.'

Jack adjusted in his seat, thinking he'd seen movement in an upstairs window. Spots of rain dotted the windscreen and Jack flicked on the wipers.

'I mean there's my parents and that's another thing entirely, but long story short, it's because of what I've seen.'

Jack turned to Cross. 'What you've seen?'

Hauntings, UFOs, that kind of thing.

'I've got what you might call a "sixth sense". I've had it ever since I was a child.'

'Sixth sense?'

'When I was seven, I saw my first ghost.'

Jack was now watching Cross. 'What happened?'

'Well, I saw an old man. He just appeared in the corner of my bedroom, but I knew I hadn't seen him walk in.'

'You don't think you could have imagined it?'

'I was scared at first. To tell my parents I mean. But rather than dismiss it my mum just said, "what did he look like?" Anyway, they got a picture from the paper, a group photo of a bunch of old boys, at some charity event, I think. There he was, in the back row. The man from my room. I picked him out from a group of about twenty. He was the man who lived in the house before my parents bought it.'

'Wasn't it scary?'

'He was a nice man. Friendly. Never spoke. Just smiled. They aren't all like that.'

'Was your mum freaked out?'

'She took the whole thing in her stride, right from the off. Very supportive the whole time. It turned out that when she was my age, that was when she started seeing things for herself.'

A shiver passed through Jack. Before he'd met Cross he thought that sort of thing was all bollocks, but Daniel Cross didn't seem the type to make things up. Even if it would help him in his career as an occult specialist.

'Every now and then I have premonitions too.'

Jack recalled the feeling that sometimes Cross was able to read his mind. His friend had this sense of knowing. But...

'How can you be sure it's not just deja vu?'

Cross looked straight ahead. 'Not everyone experiences deja vu.'

Jack whipped his head round at Cross. Another shiver passed through him. Had his own deja vu had been premonitions? Cross grinned, then pointed at the house.

'There's our man.'

Jack had taken his eye off the ball. The heavyset man from the airport was plodding along his path towards his car, his hair as jet black in broad daylight as the previous night suggested. Cross moved to his door to get out, but Jack stopped him.

'Look,' Jack said. 'His clothes.'

'No uniform.'

Last night, in the dark, they had seen a uniform. Dark jacket, dark trousers to go with the dark hair. Now he was in jeans and a shirt. Jack hoped he worked in the tower. Radar data would be solid proof of a cover up if there was one. The build of the guy told Jack it was more likely he worked security. That and that hint of recognition the night before. Jack had seen him at the airport, security was a good bet.

'Not going to work?'

'It is Sunday. Shall we see where he goes?' Jack said, feeling the smile reach his eyes.

Cross reached for his seat belt. The guy ducked into his car and they followed.

Ten minutes later, they pulled up at a supermarket.

'Wow,' Cross said. 'Tesco Express. I don't know how you stand the excitement,'

'Cheeky bastard. Come on.'

They followed him inside, hit by the smell of fresh bread

THE VANISHING OF FLIGHT 187

at the door. Shoppers ambled about picking and choosing at gap-fillers for the cupboards at home. Not Jack's man. He knew what he wanted, heading straight for the fruit and veg. Jack made his move. Basket in hand, he stood next to the security man.

'Check for spiders.'

The man turned, 'Sorry?'

Jack pointed, 'The bananas. Check for spiders.'

'Oh right,' the man said, not checking for spiders.

'Don't I know you?' Jack asked.

The man stopped. 'I don't think so.' But there was something in his voice. Doubt.

'The airport. I saw you the other day.'

'Oh,' the man smiled, relieved. 'Yeah I work security.'

'That's it.' Jack grabbed a pack of apples and placed them in his basket. 'Security.' He reached out a hand. 'Jack.'

'David.' Security man David shook his hand before reaching for a punnet of strawberries.

'Terrible business about that flight.'

David straightened up before inspecting packets of apples. 'Right. Terrible.'

'I've heard it was a hijacking...'

'Honestly? No idea.' He threw a pack of apples in his basket and moved on.

Jack followed.

'Are there any theories? I mean, you must talk about it, amongst yourselves.'

David eyed bags of mixed lettuce, doing his best to

ignore Jack. 'It's a taboo topic at work.'

'It's just that... I've got a friend; her sister was on that flight. I wish I could get some closure for her...'

David glanced at Jack, his hardened gaze softening.

'If I could speak to someone who works in the tower. You know, someone who's seen the radar. Something definitive.'

David's gaze hardened again. 'Sorry I can't be more help.'

He motioned to leave; Jack touched his arm. He stopped and glared.

'Please,' Jack reached into his pocket and pulled out a business card. All it had on there was his name and number. 'Listen, I know this is a bit much, but do you suppose you could let me know if you hear anything? Especially from the guys in the tower. It would mean a lot to my friend. Just some closure.'

David glanced around before taking the card and nodding. 'I'll see what I can do.'

Jack stood and watched as David hurried away.

10

The grey skies had finally produced the rain they'd been threatening all morning, a grim backdrop to the news playing in the background, just treading over the same ground as before. No new developments. No wreckage found. Just a flight that might as well have vanished into thin air, leaving loved ones on the ground in limbo. Jack and Cross were sitting in the living room, a laptop a piece, trying to find a link between the passengers, hoping to reveal anything to account for the flight's disappearance.

They'd already been fishing about in Adam Shepherd's background, to see if that threw up any red flags. Adam was an entrepreneur with a background in start-up businesses who eventually moved into railways and saw a gap in the airline market. People rarely get to where Adam Shepherd was without treading on a few toes, but nothing in his background suggested he might have anything to do with the flight going missing. And while someone with Adam's background might be familiar with the inside of a courtroom, they would hardly qualify as a target for terror. All in all, for all they could tell, Adam Shepherd was clean.

Cross had suggested there might be a link between some of the passengers. That it could be better for some powerful group if the flight disappeared. He mentioned one case where a group of researchers on the verge of some major medical breakthrough were on a flight that was targeted by terror. It wasn't much, but Jack thought this theory could hold water. He didn't like coincidences. Little Green Men was a stretch too far, but earthly greed… That was something all too plausible. They'd split the passenger list in two and were working their way through it. Jack was about halfway through his list.

'Anything so far?' Jack asked.

'A couple here and there who work together, but nothing significant. You?'

'Same.'

The work was dull but necessary. In a few hours, he'd be calling Ruth Draper with an update and hoped to have a little more than airport staff acting suspiciously. The passenger list and cross-checking each individual's info turned up zero. There were no persons of interest on board, no millionaires, no cancer cure. No parties bigger than two that they could see, and they were all working for run-of-the-mill companies. Cross was struck by inspiration and darted back to his laptop. Jack combed over his notes again to see if there was anything he'd missed, all the while, ears glued to the television expecting the break in the case that would end Ruth's interest. Yesterday morning, he might have welcomed it.

Cross had only been working on his new idea for a couple of minutes before calling Jack over. Jack stared over Cross's shoulder at a website loaded with flight data info.

'Look at this... We've got crash info, black box recordings...'

'Is that legal?'

'That's just it,' Cross said looking up at Jack, 'everything on this page has come from Freedom of Information Act requests.'

Jack nodded, impressed with his friend's work.

'More than that...' he said clicking onto another page, 'It isn't just info from the black boxes. It says here that the plane and engine manufacturers all put transmitters into anything they build.'

'So it's not just the er, flight data recorders that give this info?'

'There's military radar on here and all sorts. What do you think?' Cross looked up again, hopeful.

Jack smiled. 'I think we've got a new line of enquiry. I'll find out who made the plane and engines, you try to get hold of the military r—'

The phone on Jack's desk burst into its shrill ring.

'Try to get hold of the military radar,' Jack finished before answering the phone. 'Hello?' Jack said. 'Hello?' he said again, more forcefully now.

Cross glanced over from the settee. Jack never gave his name or business when he answered the phone. Whoever was on the line would have to announce himself if he wanted Jack's help. Finally, someone spoke.

'They're lying.'

'Who is this?'

'They're lying about the flight.'

'David? Is that you?'

There was a click at the other end and the phone went dead. Jack quickly dialled to see if whoever had called had forgotten to block their number. No such luck. He placed the receiver back into the cradle.

Jack grabbed his jacket. 'I'm going out.'

CHAPTER THREE

THE WINDSCREEN WIPERS slashed through the rain as Jack sped towards David's house. There had been little time between David taking Jack's business card and the call itself, which made him the most likely culprit. With Cross back at the flat filing Freedom of Information requests, Jack was flying solo.

Cross seemed to be enjoying the detective work, even the dull, waiting around parts. Having Cross around again was a calming influence, and despite the fact they didn't feel the need to fill the silence with constant chatter, his presence made normally boring parts of the job less painful. Not only that, but he threw himself into research.

Jack hurled the car around the corner into David's street. The heavy rain had kept everybody bar one stubborn dog-walker indoors, the black clouds making it easy to spot who was watching early evening television. That included David. At least he was in. Jack marched along the path, turning his collar to the rain. Jack banged on the door.

The door swung open. David was shocked. He stood half hidden behind the door, using it as a shield. 'You? What are you doing here?'

'Did you call me about the flight?'

David's frown deepened and his cheeks took on a red colour. 'How did you know where I lived?'

Jack stepped back slightly, 'I've just got a call, was it from you?'

'I said, how do you know where I live?'

Jack realised that it wasn't anger provoking these reactions. It was fear.

'Get off my doorstep or I'm calling the police.'

The security guard cut an imposing figure, he'd been in his fair share of battles no doubt. To see him rattled like this unsettled Jack.

'Answer my questions and you'll never see me again.'

'I never called you...' he glanced out into the street before lowering his voice. 'I spoke to a friend. He works in the tower. It must have been him. Now, get off my doorstep.'

Jack frowned. 'What are you afraid of?'

'Look, don't come back here. I'll speak to my friend. Get him to call you.'

Jack took a step back. 'Two days. If I haven't heard anything in two days, I'll be back.

David nodded from behind the door and slammed it shut.

Jack turned and jogged back to his car. Rain pounded off the roof while he stared at Ruth Draper's business card. He dialled her number, pausing before he called.

His run in with the flight attendants showed there was something going on. *It wasn't a crash.* And David was clearly worried about some sort of repercussions. From whom? The first person to come to Jack's mind was Mr MI5. Had the airport staff been told to keep schtum about the flight? Being told that directly by someone from MI5 would arouse suspicion. A meeting like that would do nothing but set tongues wagging. Rather than being told to shut up, it might have been a brief that went between the airport staff. Say nothing at all. Not even to each other. Non-disclosure agreements. Compartmentalisation. Maybe someone had already spoken out and been made an example of. Something was going on, and perhaps the next move if the phone call from the mystery tower worker failed to materialise was to put pressure on Adam Shepherd himself.

Jack hit dial and called Ruth. She picked up straight away.

'Ruth? Jack. I'm starting to think that you were right. As I said before, getting concrete proof won't be easy, but we've got a couple of irons in the fire and unless there are any official announcements, I should be able to give you another update in 48 hours.'

'I appreciate all you're doing,' Ruth said.

There was a pause and it sounded to Jack like she wanted to say more. He waited.

'There is one more thing...' Ruth said eventually. 'This will sound like I'm losing my mind, but I have to say it.'

Jack stayed silent again, not wanting to lead or dissuade her from continuing.

'I have a feeling that Hannah is still alive.'

Jack's stomach sank. The hope of relatives in cases like this could either get them through the difficulty or drive them mad. He desperately wanted closure for Ruth, because the hope she was holding on to was the bad kind. This was the part of the job he disliked the most. There was no point sugar coating it.

'Ruth, you have to prepare yourself for the chance, the *probability* that Hannah is gone. A flight missing for more than 48 hours... the more time passes, the less likely it is we'll hear good news. I just want you to be ready for that.'

'I'm not crazy.'

Jack didn't want to get into an argument about how dead Hannah was. Arguing was only going to make things worse.

'I'll speak to you in 48 hours.'

Jack ended the call and sat for a moment, listening to the drumbeat of rain before firing the car into life. He pulled away and headed back the way he came, eager to tell Cross the news of the tower worker. If David had been lying, the time to say so would have been when Jack threatened to return. If it was David who'd made the call, he'd have told Jack everything just to get him off his doorstep. Jack reached a junction and glanced in the mirror.

That was when he noticed the car following him.

2

The streetlights flickered to life as Jack Talbot sat at the traffic lights, his wipers clearing the windscreen of the downpour. His eyes were still on the black saloon car two cars back. He wasn't sure if they knew he'd spotted them, or if he was supposed to have seen them, but for the last three turns he'd taken, they had taken the same, waiting for Jack to indicate before doing so themselves. Through the beams of their lights, it was difficult to see who was driving, or if they were alone, but Jack had the feeling there would be more than one person in the car. The car behind honked his horn and Jack glanced up to see the light now green.

He thought about waiting until the light changed back to red and taking off just before it did; or indicating to turn and going on, just to be sure they were following. In the end he did neither, setting off slowly and waving a hand of apology behind. There was no need to make sure they were following; he knew it as fact. He sped up, just to see if they did the same. Jack was leading them. What he didn't want to do was to lead them straight to his door. The tail had latched on at David's place, so there was a chance they didn't know where he lived. As the single lane became three, he glanced again into the mirror. They'd taken the bait.

He weaved through the rain-speckled beams of light from the traffic. Most likely the tail was someone from the airline keeping tabs on anyone poking around asking too many questions. If they found his place, they'd have the upper hand - they already knew his number plate. Jack slowed slightly and eyed the approaching exit. He watched for his new friends pulling into his lane, trapping them behind the following car and then waited. The exit neared but he needed a gap in the lanes to his left. At the last moment one appeared, and he wrenched the wheel hard, dragging him through speeding traffic. The wheels almost came from under the rear of the car, threatening to overtake the front end as they slid on the slick surface. Jack corrected the steering and pressed the pedal to the floor, tyres screaming along the exit.

Horns blared as he left the main road behind, entering the relative remoteness of the industrial estate.

Old warehouses loomed around him, mostly disused, sad evidence of the good old days his dad would talk about whenever he got the chance. The road here was straight, arrowing between warehouses and wire fences, and Jack threw another glance in the mirror.

Nothing.

He allowed himself a congratulatory smile, which faded as the exit road behind glistened in twin beams of silver light. Jack killed the lights on his own car and yanked the wheel hard, turning him straight into the lot of a salvage yard. He turned full circle, with the entrance now slightly behind him on his right. He threw the car into reverse, hoping he'd get back in time to hide, parking behind a fence panel. In the pitch black of the yard, Jack sat and waited.

Between the corrugated panels of the entrance, Jack could see nothing more than a few yards of pot-holed road, rain pelting the surface. The sheets of rain before him lit up, and before long the road too, shadows growing in the potholes, but the car that had followed him from David's was no longer speeding after him. Now, it moved at a crawl, lights in front joined by the pencil thin beam of a torch. The torch swept from the passenger window. Jack held the key between finger and thumb, ready to fire the car into life. He waited. The car stopped.

The torch beam swept back and forth. From the narrow angle he had, he couldn't see if the downpour had covered his tracks. All he could do was hope.

'Come on. Come on. Just fuck off.'

The beam swept again back and forth into the yard, then down at the road. It lifted again into the yard. Jack held his breath. Then, just as he thought they'd leave, the torch beam went out. Jack didn't know if they were getting ready to go or preparing to investigate on foot. Jack gripped the key, his foot poised over the pedal.

Anyone walking through that gate is getting run over.

What were they waiting for? Then, movement. The beams of light edged forward, and Jack finally saw the car. It stopped again. Eyes glued to the car, Jack leaned across to the glove box and reached inside. He placed the cosh on the seat beside him, reassured by the heft of it. Just at the moment Jack expected to see the torch beam, or the door open, the car eased forward, before taking off into the night. Jack waited before starting his own car.

'Message received.'

3

'I've been on about doing it for a while now,' Jack said to Cross as they pulled up outside.

It was a ten-minute drive from Jack's flat, but ten minutes too short to escape that air of danger, even in the morning light. The kind of place you double check you've locked your car (after making sure there's nothing on display, lest ye lose a window), before reluctantly walking away to take care of your unsavoury business. The sort of place where the sight of another person makes you feel worse, not better.

'It's not the nicest place, but it'll be better than running my business from my flat.'

Jack had arrived home to a frantic Daniel Cross the night before explaining his run-in with whoever the hell it was tailing him from David's place, before outlining the need to separate his private and business lives, something he might have done a lot earlier, if he'd had the money.

'You didn't like the first place?' Cross said, in a tone that suggested all was not lost.

Jack shook his head, 'Did you see the rent on that place? I'd still like to eat. If it weren't for Ruth Draper paying me a week at a time, I wouldn't be looking here.'

They buzzed the door and waited for the estate agent to appear.

'You know, your money would go a lot further up north...' Cross said, planting a seed.

'What? Where you are?'

'Just saying. I could even throw a little business your way, every now and again.'

Jack pondered for a moment.

Hauntings and UFOs.

A small involuntary shake of the head chased the thought away. 'Let's just see what this place is like.'

The estate agent came to the door. A young, smiling man, eager to please.

He talked in an unending stream, seemingly without punctuation, highlighting the space (it was cramped), kitchen amenities (in need of a good clean), and great location (see above).

When the moment came for Jack to get a word in edgeways, he took his chance. 'That's great, thanks very much. Could you give us a moment?'

The estate agent nodded and smiled again, this one masking here-we-go-again disappointment, before excusing himself and saying he'd wait outside.

'Nice kid,' Cross said.

Jack nodded, 'Wonder how many times he's tried to polish this turd. I almost feel bad for him.'

'With a good clean...' Cross offered.

'No, no, I'm not dismissing it. Like you say...' Jack looked around, trying to visualise what the small space would look like with his desk and files crammed in there, 'with a good clean...'

'So, where are we?' Cross asked.

Jack sighed, 'I'll probably take it.'

'I meant with the case.'

Jack turned, distracted from his visualisation. 'Oh right. Dead end really. Nobody on board of any significance, you spent all last night digging into Adam Shepherd - thanks for that, by the way – and he's as clean as a whistle. I suppose we're sitting on our hands until your FOIA requests come back, or David's friend in the tower gets in touch. I think another visit to David will hurry that along.'

Cross went to the window and peered down into the street. 'Well, they're hiding something, that's for sure.'

'Going to a lot of trouble to do it too, if my experience last night is anything to go by,' Jack replied.

'Why though?'

Jack opened a cupboard and regretted it, quickly closing the smell back inside. 'Protecting the share price?'

'You think that's all it is?' Cross asked.

'I don't see what else it could be,' Jack said motioning towards the door, 'Come on.'

Cross stopped Jack, 'This might sound mad, but last night I was researching unusual flights. Flights that just dropped off the face of the earth. If we could get someone who's seen the radar...'

'Let me guess. You think the Bermuda Triangle has migrated Christ knows how many miles and—'

'There have been cases where pilots have been involved in near-misses with UFOs and—'

'UFOs?'

'Hear me out. If there was some sort of incident where unknown technology somehow collided with a passenger plane, wouldn't there be a plot to keep that quiet? Wouldn't military intelligence be involved? Or what if it had been hijacked? The whole plane. Taken by a UFO.'

Jack eyed Cross, 'Let's keep our suggestions earthly for now, eh? It's much more likely it's been nabbed by bad earthlings; some procedural guideline's been overlooked, and Mr Shepherd is doing his best to avoid a shedload of Ruth Drapers.'

'I don't think we should dismiss it. It does fit with

everything that's happened.'

Jack nodded. 'You're right. But let's just wait and see what our man in the tower has to—'

Jack's phone buzzed. He and Cross exchanged a glance. Could it be the man from the tower already? Jack read the caller ID. His shoulders slumped.

'Hello, Damien.'

Cross's body language mirrored Jack's and they traipsed downstairs. Jack stopped dead in the cool staircase and held up a hand to Cross.

'Say that again...'

Cross frowned and shrugged.

Jack felt the colour draining from his face. 'It can't be, that's impossible... No, I'll be there. See you soon.'

He ended the call and dropped his phone back into his pocket before slowly turning to Cross.

'You're not gonna believe this.'

4

The Shepherd Airlines crisis management team were back in the meeting room at the airport. The room was silent. The three of them paced trying to understand exactly what was going on. The bookish woman turned to her colleagues. Jason had barely said a word since this thing had started, so expecting him to speak now was a stretch. But Tony? She struggled to recall a time he was lost for words. His eyes were distant, unfocused, like he was trying to come to grips with what they'd just seen.

'Okay, I'm just going to come out and say it...' The others never moved, but she knew they'd heard her. 'Have you ever seen anything like this?'

Her question was met with silence. She turned to her colleagues one by one, and each turned back and shook his head.

'Well we need to figure something—'

'There's no protocol for this!'

It was Jason. The loudness of his interruption snapped everyone from their daze.

'Great. That's what you can tell Adam. He'll be here any second.'

Tony mumbled. 'The media have already got wind of this. There's blood in the water.'

'Guys, come on.' What they needed now was focus. 'Forget the media, we've got something much bigger to deal with. What are we going to—'

Too late. The double doors flew open and Adam Shepherd burst in. As always, he was dressed in a clean pressed suit, but that did little to hide his panic. He dabbed at a nick on his cheek with his handkerchief. He'd probably been shaving when he heard the news. His beleaguered assistant trailed in his wake, a clueless expression on her face suggesting she knew even less than everyone else in the room. She closed the doors behind them, and Adam stood at the table leaning on one of the chairs, eyes flitting between each person in the room. The heavy silence remained.

THE VANISHING OF FLIGHT 187

'Well?!' he boomed, 'Somebody fucking speak.'

She'd never heard Adam swear.

Tony's eyes shifted from one colleague to another, but nobody spoke. He finally stepped forward. 'I'm not sure who told the press—'

'The press?! Fuck the press! What the hell happened to my plane?'

Tony turned to his left, 'Jason. Jason? What do we know so far?'

Jason was older than Tony and lacked his calm at the best of times, but this latest development with 187 had left him clearly rattled. It was the first time Adam had heard him speak and he was probably starting to wonder what exactly it was he did.

Jason cleared his throat. 'A little under one hour ago, air traffic control reported an incident over the English Channel. A near-miss. A flight on its way to Brussels involved with…'

Adam raised his eyebrows, encouraging him to continue. He did not. Angela did.

'It was Flight 187, sir.'

Adam's face dropped. '*My* 187?'

She nodded. 'They confirmed with ATC. ATC asked them for fuel status. Once that was established, they were told to return.'

'Return?'

'Here.'

Adam's eyebrows raised. 'Flight 187… is here.'

'That's right,' Tony said.

'As of when?'

'It landed twenty minutes ago.'

Adam took a deep breath and turned to his assistant.

'Karen, would you go and get us some coffee? And one for yourself.'

She nodded and left the room, nobody speaking until the doors were closed behind her.

Adam rubbed at his forehead. 'What about the passengers?'

'We don't know.'

'Where had it been?'

'We don't know.'

'But the pilots are okay?'

'Yes, sir. Well enough to speak with the tower. Well enough to land...'

Adam turned to the window and stared at normality outside, no doubt wishing he could be part of it. That wasn't going to happen. This was going to be a long day, for all of them.

Tony asked, 'Sir, what would you like us to tell the press?'

Adam whipped around. 'That's what I pay *you* for. The first thing we need to do is make sure—'

The phone on the table started to ring.

Adam continued, 'Is to make sure that everyone on board is...' He tailed off and his eyes flickered like he was recalling the last time that phone rang. Tony answered, before offering the receiver to Adam.

'It's for you.'

Adam loosened his collar.

'Who is it?'

Tony asked the caller.

'He won't say. He says you know who he is.'

Adam swayed and his mouth moved like a fish on a riverbank. He knew who it was all right. He just wished it were someone else. After a moment, Adam pulled the phone away from his face. 'Could you give me the room? Find Karen at the coffee shop. I'll call her when I need you.'

Everyone silently filed from the room and Angela glanced at Adam as she closed the doors. His eyes told her Adam wanted them to stay. The last thing he wanted was to be left alone in the room with this. But that wasn't going to happen.

Through the closing doors she saw him put the phone back to his ear. 'Okay, they're gone... Yes, I'll wait.'

5

Adam Shepherd paced nervously. It had only been a few minutes since he'd cleared the meeting room, but whatever was coming next was taking far too long. He tried imagining what was going on in the outside world, and what that might lead to. The disbelief, the press speculation, share price falls, reputation damage. If he had to wait in here another minute, he might go mad.

He whipped round at the sound of the door opening and

froze in place. A handsome man appeared in a business suit.

'Mr Shepherd?'

Adam nodded.

'Please, follow me.'

Without objection, Adam Shepherd followed the young man from the room, but instead of turning left and into the airport proper, they turned right into a long, narrow corridor. Adam glanced back over his shoulder, longingly eyeing the normal world that went about its business without him. They barely noticed he'd gone. That's what scared him. He turned back and trotted to make up the space between him and the young man.

'Where are we going?' he asked, voice faint.

The young man didn't look back and it was only now that Adam realised he'd be hard pressed to give a description of him. His legs felt weak, and now the thoughts and ideas coming to him were worse than share prices and ruined reputation.

Suddenly, the young man stopped. He turned to his left, still not looking at Adam, and knocked. In the wall, there was a door, unmarked,

'Come!'

The young man opened the door and stepped aside. Adam stepped forward and peered into the room. This was a smaller meeting room than the airport had given him use of, just a round table and four chairs. Only one chair was occupied. Adam Shepherd felt that same dislike for the man sitting in it as he did the first time they met. He was middle-aged, stern, with a thin face, absorbed in the file before him.

THE VANISHING OF FLIGHT 187

Adam still had the impression that the man was connected to the military. Before he knew it, he was standing by the table and the door closed behind him.

'Sit.'

Adam sat opposite the man who finally looked up. The man smiled, but rather than soften his features it made Adam think of a shark.

'What can you tell me?'

'Tell you?'

'What can you tell me about the flight?'

'We've been over this—'

'No. Things have changed. Tell me.'

'The flight that went missing last Thursday night has returned.'

'Go on.'

'Sorry, you know what? No.'

'No?'

'I want answers. Who are you?'

The man smiled that unlikeable smile again. 'I'm working with the government. Go on.'

'If you work for the government, you must have an ID badge.'

The man's jaw clenched. He took a breath, 'I'm here to help. To make your problem disappear.'

When the last word came out, his glare hardened as if to say the same could happen to him.

Adam stared back at him, holding eye contact though all he wanted was to look away. Anywhere but into those empty eyes. 'Let's not fuck around here, you're not here for *me*. You're here for *you*. You're here for you, or you wouldn't be here at all. If you want my cooperation, you'll show me your badge.'

He reached into his pocket, flipped open a wallet and slid his ID across the table. 'That's the stress talking, so I'll let it slide. Once.'

'Adrian Grieve,' Adam read out.

Grieve snatched the wallet back and pocketed it. 'Good. Now we're not fucking around... tell me what else you know.'

Adam shrugged. 'I don't know anything else.'

'The passengers? Are they alive?'

'Alive? Well, yes... I mean... I think so.'

'I'll find out if you're lying.'

'Why would I lie?'

Grieve was looking at a file. He removed a photograph. 'I'd hate for anything to happen to Katie.'

Adam broke out in a cold sweat. He never thought there could be a threat to his daughter. She was

out of sight, out of mind

away at boarding school. He swallowed hard, hoping to swallow the sickness he felt with it.

'I swear. I'm telling you everything.'

Grieve stood up and paced the short distance between the walls, prowling like a caged animal. 'So you know less than I do. That works.' He seemed slightly relieved to Adam, and his voice took on more authority when he spoke again. 'The flight is being held on the runway. The passengers and crew will be checked—'

'Checked?'

'We have a medical team on standby. They'll be debriefed, and then they'll be free to go.'

'What does that mean? Debriefed? Where have they been? What am I going to tell the press?'

'You're to say nothing. When we've completed our tests, the passengers will be released, and your team will be given a prepared statement...'

'The press won't just let this go—'

'The press...'

Adrian Grieve stopped pacing and turned to Adam with a look that turned him cold.

'...will have something else to talk about soon enough, don't you worry...neither yourself nor your team will do or say anything beyond that statement. Is that clear?'

Adam Shepherd nodded. Now the adrenaline had worn off, his hands shook. Grieve opened the door and the stark corridor outside was in darkness. Adam stood, nodded, and left. Keep silent and Katie will be fine. But there was one more question. He turned back just before the door closed.

'What about my airline?'

Grieve stared for a second before speaking, and in that second Adam got the impression that the door would simply close. Conversation over. If that's what happened, he'd be fine with it.

'Do as we say, Mr Shepherd, and your airline will be fine.'

The door closed and, in the darkness, Adam saw a shape.

He jumped and stifled a scream before realising that the shape was the young man in the suit, waiting to escort him back. Without a word he set off and Adam followed, the airport terminal coming into sight at the end of the corridor, that patch of daily life and normality tantalisingly within reach.

Outside the meeting room, they stopped, and the young man turned to face him. 'You're to wait in here until further notice. I'll let the others know they can return.'

He opened the door and Adam stepped inside. Adam turned to close the door and was surprised to see the young man still standing there. He regarded Adam with that same cold stare Adrian Grieve had.

'Your meeting just now... It never happened. Is that clear?'

Adam just nodded and stepped back, relieved when the doors finally closed, and he was left alone.

6

As Adam Shepherd was in a meeting that never happened, Jack and Cross were standing on Ruth Draper's doorstep. High midday sun beat down upon them, their shadows a tiny puddle at their feet. Jack knocked on the door.

'What if she's not in?' Cross asked.

'I don't think she'll be at work. She comes across as the strong type, but there's someone in there who's worried sick about her sister. She's at home.'

THE VANISHING OF FLIGHT 187

Jack knocked on the door again, harder this time. An outline filled the panels of frosted glass.

'Mr Talbot… What are you doing here?'

Rather than waste time explaining how he, a detective, found out where she lived, Jack instead cut to the much more important chase. 'The flight. It's back.'

'Back?'

'Hannah's flight landed back here about an hour ago…'

Ruth Draper's eyes filled with tears.

'I want to set your expectations here, Ruth. We don't know any more than that. We don't know who's on board, who isn't, what state they're in… But it's something. Get your coat, we'll take you to the airport.'

Ruth nodded vacantly and stood in a daze; eyes unfocused like she didn't believe this was happening. Jack couldn't blame her. It felt to him like he was in the grip of a dream. With a tiny shake of the head Ruth's eyes cleared and she turned and grabbed a light jacket.

'I've been watching the news; they didn't say anything.' She stepped from the house before dashing back in to grab her keys.

'I imagine they can't,' Cross said.

'We have a contact in the media. He said they're being told to keep quiet, but it's real,' Jack said, watching Ruth lock the door with a trembling hand.

The three of them marched back along the path drenched in sunshine and Jack opened the door for Ruth. She looked like a woman who expected to wake up at any moment. Jack climbed into the car, glancing at Cross as he did. From the look on his friend's face, the three of them had a similar feeling.

They drove to the airport in silence. Ruth asked Jack to turn on the lunchtime news, but when the top story was more non-news about politics she asked him to turn it off again. As the green surroundings gave way to the grey and white building of the airport terminal, Jack spotted the throng of news people at the door again. Fewer than the night of the disappearance - word must still have been getting out. They parked up and headed into the building, forcing through the crowds and flashbulbs until they were inside.

The terminal building again had that strange air about it. Everyone there knew they were in the middle of something truly extraordinary and Jack recalled the 9/11 this-isn't-really-happening confusion. The air was a buzz of excited chatter that had been absent earlier and only now did Jack realise just how quiet it had been a few hours before. Jack threw a cursory glance at the arrivals board, wondering if Flight 187 had made an appearance there, but of course there was nothing that would fuel such expectations.

'Let's get these seats, while they're still here,' Cross said gesturing at an empty row of chairs.

They moved across and Ruth said absently, 'I'm not sure I can sit.'

'Daniel's right,' Jack said. 'This place is filling up fast. We've got no idea what's going on or how long it could take...' Jack eyed the surroundings, looking for any familiar face who could perhaps shed light on their unusual situation. There was no-one, but he knew where there might be.

'Wait here, I'm er... going for a walk.'

Cross nodded helping the dazed and confused Ruth into her seat. Jack headed further into the airport. For security.

The security area lay before him - eight conveyor belts, two either side of four walk-through metal-detectors.

'Have you got your boarding card?' came the voice again, this time more curtly than the first.

'I haven't got a passport, I'm not flying,' Jack said absently, scanning beyond the rope maze that led to the crowds of nervous passengers.

'Could you step aside then, sir?'

Jack finally looked at the airport employee, a short, stocky man, perma-smile plastered on his face despite his chagrin.

'Right. Sorry.' Jack turned to the older couple behind him. 'Sorry.'

They smiled as they went past but Jack was already looking back into the security area, looking through the glass wall for the burly man with jet-black hair. By this time, word of the flight would have spread through the staff like wildfire, and David would be a good place to start if he wanted answers.

His eyes found him, checking bags and coats were placed correctly into trays at the far end, that same look on his face as everyone else's – shell-shocked disbelief. Every couple of seconds he'd disappear behind the shuffling bodies of passengers removing belts and unpacking cosmetics. The queue was double digit and growing - new passengers joining his line before filtering to the shorter queues.

Jack moved off to his left to get a direct view of the security lane, hoping to catch David's eye. He stood for a minute, just staring, an older couple beside him cooing and waving at the younger couple going away to wherever, strangely oblivious to the bizarre events unfolding around them.

Just as Jack was about to give up, David glanced upward, shoulders sinking on sight of the pestering detective. David turned back to see if anyone had noticed his pause, then looked back at Jack, holding up two fingers. Jack nodded. He paced back and forth until David spoke to his supervisor. A slight tilt of his head gestured at Jack to move to his right and Jack followed him with his eyes as he emerged back through the security entrance and out into the main terminal building. Jack followed him all the way to the gents.

Inside, the men's room was crowded, and Jack caught sight of David entering one of the stalls. Jack waited outside the closed door, hoping no-one would care he wasn't taking the other empty stall. After a moment, the toilet flushed and David emerged, clicking his ballpoint pen and sliding it back into his shirt pocket. With a nod, he was gone, and Jack entered the stall. There was a note waiting for him, scrawled on toilet paper.

"They're alive. That's all I know. Please leave me alone."

THE VANISHING OF FLIGHT 187

7

By the time Jack arrived back in departures, Daniel Cross was standing with Damien. Jack's eyes flashed to the seats and he was relieved to see Ruth Draper sitting there, that glazed look of disbelief still plastered on her face.

Jack weaved between the passengers trailing this way and that and sat beside her. 'I have good news. I've just spoken to a contact about the passengers. They're alive.'

A tiny cry escaped, and Ruth hugged him. She cried into his shoulder gently.

'That's all I know for now, but it's something.'

'Thank you.' The voice was fragile and tiny, a far cry from the person in his office on Friday morning.

Jack caught Cross's eye and waved him over. As Cross made his way back, Jack turned to Ruth.

'You alright?'

Jack felt the nod on his shoulder before Ruth pulled away and dabbed at her eyes with a sleeve.

'I just need to talk to Daniel for a moment and then he'll come and sit with you. Okay?'

Ruth nodded and fished in her bag, removing a tissue with a flourish like it was a magic trick. Jack placed a hand on her upper arm.

'Will you be okay while I have a word with Danny?'

She nodded, dabbing at her eyes. Jack rose at met Cross a few feet from Ruth, just out of earshot.

'What's going on?' Cross asked.

'Spoke to our friend in security. They're alive.'

'All of them?'

'That's what he said.' Jack looked across and Damien lifted a hand in a wave. Jack mirrored the gesture. 'What's Damien saying?'

'Not a lot really. He heard from someone who heard from the tower that the flight was back. They're holding it on the runway. Or at least, they were.'

'Okay. I'll have a word with him. Are you okay to sit with Ruth for a minute?'

'Sure,' Cross said without pause.

Before he could go Jack asked, 'How are you enjoying your trip so far?'

'Never a dull moment.' Cross smiled and strode to the seats where Ruth awaited.

Jack approached Damien, who as always, was wearing his trademark green jacket. 'You ever take this thing off?' Jack smiled.

'How would you find me otherwise?' Damien shrugged back. 'Heard anything?'

'Just that everyone on board is alive. No updates other than that... Thanks for that passenger list by the way.'

'Usual deal. Get me a story and we'll call it quits,' he grinned.

'What have you got so far?' Jack asked.

'Not a lot. Everyone's been tight lipped about this one.'

'Tell me about it.'

'All I can say for sure at this point is that they've been

hiding something.'

Jack nodded. 'We went through your list with a fine-toothed comb. Couldn't find anything interesting on the passengers though.'

Damien shook his head. 'No.' He nudged Jack's arm and gestured at Cross, 'Your friend's a character.'

'What do you mean?'

'He was asking if I had a contact in the tower who could get radar. Thinks it might be a UFO.'

Jack looked at Cross himself. He was comforting Ruth with that easy-going warmth he had with people. He certainly made an impression.

'You know,' he said to Damien, 'the longer this goes on the weirder it gets.'

'What? You don't mean...' Damien scoffed. 'Little Green Men, Jack?'

'I'm just saying...' Jack cast his mind back to the previous winter in North Yorkshire, 'Stranger things have happened.'

Damien laughed. When he realised Jack wasn't joking, he stopped.

8

The sun had gone down, and the terminal building had filled with reporters and interested parties like moths drawn to electric lighting. The air was filled with rumour and speculation and it seemed everyone had their own separate theory on exactly what it was that was going on. Jack and

Damien had spent time here or there trying to get more information but came away with only more conjecture.

Stories that it was a hijacking and that some passengers were dead were the most common, to the extent that Jack and Damien were starting to believe it themselves, despite what David said, after all, what else could be taking so long? Either way, Jack had decided to leave security guy David alone. Whatever was going on, it had given airport employees more than a little cause for concern, David included.

David had been good enough to give him the most important information, even if it was just to get rid of him, and Jack had to respect that. The last thing he wanted on his quest for answers was to endanger anyone. Chances were, the call from his friend in the tower would not materialise, but, now that the flight was back, it didn't really matter.

None of it did. As soon as Hannah walked out of the airport with Ruth, the subject, and the case, would be closed. There would be an official statement tying everything into a neat little bow, and that would be that. Even if that statement wasn't the whole truth, there was a part of him that wanted to be done with it. It was a case that he was reluctant to take from the off. He'd collect a cheque from Ruth for services rendered and use that for a deposit on a real office, then he could get back to real cases. Ones less weird. Ones where he wouldn't be followed by mystery men.

Cross had seemed to enjoy himself, even if he had spent the last few hours in an airport with no intention of flying anywhere. Poor guy had extended his visit by an extra day and ended up spending most of that day babysitting a grown woman in a departures lounge.

Movement caught Jack's eye to his left and he and Cross turned. A crowd was shuffling as if remote controlled towards the security area. He glanced back at Damien who called across as he went by.

'Presser. Speak to you after.'

Jack nodded and raised a hand. He had a feeling that as soon as the press were out of the way, the passengers would be released. They'd been here for hours, though all parties were too excited and nervous to think about eating or sleep.

'Won't be long now,' Jack smiled at Ruth.

Jack's concerns about the dead hostage rumours had faded after he came back to Ruth and Cross. Cross had a way of sensing things, and his face said that whatever happened, they'd be walking out of that airport with Hannah in tow.

At once, all eyes remaining in the arrivals area were drawn to the double doors marked arrivals. They burst open and tired passengers ran into the arms of awaiting friends and family. A few photographers and cameramen had waited behind, blasting the returning travellers in harsh white light. The air was filled with joyous screams and tears and laughter.

Ruth stood and made her way on uneasy feet to the entrance, awaiting sight of Hannah. Jack recognised Hannah's friend Nicola as she ran to the arms of her tearful parents. Nicola and Hannah must have got separated along the way as the latter was nowhere in sight. Ruth was on tiptoe, leaning this way and that to get an angle through the crowds, hoping to spot her sister. Jack looked at Ruth, then at Cross, before trying to spot Hannah himself. Again, Cross's face said that it would be a matter of time before she appeared, and then, as the crowd of returnees thinned out, there was Hannah. Tired, pale, but alive. She sprinted as soon as she saw Ruth and burst into tears in her sister's arms.

After a few minutes, the four of them left the airport together. A happy ending to a strange case. Or so Jack thought. In truth, it was just beginning.

9

The car journey back to Ruth's place was silent like the night. The four passengers trying to contemplate what had happened. As they'd approached the car, Ruth had asked what exactly had gone on, only for Hannah to shut her down with a swift rebuke. Jack and Cross had exchanged a look but nothing more and on they had gone. Around five minutes before they arrived at Ruth's house, Jack's phone vibrated. It was a call from Damien. He let go to voicemail.

In Ruth's street, lights were on in the neighbour's houses, despite the hour. The four of them got out and Ruth led her sister to the front door and they both disappeared inside.

Jack and Cross made their way back to the car.

Cross turned to Jack, 'Well. That was interesting.'

'Glad you stayed the extra day?' Jack asked.

'I could stay longer...'

'What do you—'

Cross pointed and Jack turned to see Ruth striding back

down the path. Ruth Draper's expression was one of stiff resolve.

Jack had feared this might happen. 'Ruth, you've got your sister back, shaken, but alive and in time, she'll be well.'

'We're not finished,' she said.

'I don't really see how much more—'

'The proof I asked for. The case isn't closed. They're still hiding something, and I still intend to find out exactly what it is. If you can't help me—'

Jack stepped forward, 'It's not that I can't help you. I just want to prepare you for the fact that the chances of this coming to a conclusion that you find satisfactory—'

'Your reputation? Is that what you're worried about?'

Jack frowned. 'That's offensive. Besides, in this line of work you haven't got much else.'

'How long?'

'What?'

'How long would it take, to come to a satisfactory conclusion?'

'Ruth, it could take weeks. It could take months. It may never happen at all.'

Ruth Draper pulled her phone out of her pocket to check the date. 'You've got one week.'

'What?'

'One week. Come back to me with what you have. We'll review. If it's worth pursuing, we'll extend. If not, we go our separate ways. Get me something concrete, I'll pay you for a month. Would you consider that fair, Mr Talbot?'

Jack glanced over at Cross whose face suggested he was enjoying this far too much. Jack's look asked if Cross might extend his stay another week. Cross slowly nodded.

Jack held out a hand, 'Very fair.'

Ruth Draper shook it.

'I don't want to be a pest, obviously Hannah's got some recovering to do, but I'd like to call in tomorrow, just to see how she's doing.'

Ruth smiled a tired, but genuine smile. 'That would be fine. Thank you Mr Talbot. Mr Cross.'

Jack and Cross both nodded their goodbyes and Ruth headed back to the house. As soon as she was inside, Jack and Cross got back into the car.

Cross turned to Jack, 'So what happens now?'

'We'll head back to HQ, gather what we've got, and work out our next steps... And maybe have a cheeky drink.'

Cross smiled. 'Sounds like a plan.'

Back at Jack's place he'd called Damien, who said that there was nothing he could say outside of the press conference footage that had been playing on a loop since they'd returned. The official story was a hijacking that had taken the plane to a remote island, and that the government had been negotiating over the past few days for the safe return of the passengers, all of whom had been unharmed. There was the official statement, and that was that. No questions, despite the assembled media having many, and Damien said that to the best of his knowledge, the mystery military man had not been in attendance.

'Did you believe it?' Cross asked.

'Honestly,' Damien said, 'not a word. I mean...'

Jack was now sitting at his desk, taking notes.

'...where was the plane? Wherever it was, nobody at the other end knew it was missing? Who took it and what did they want? There are way more questions than answers.'

'Anyone got any theories as to what really happened?' Jack asked, trying his best not to look at Cross, whose crazy UFO story was gaining traction by the second.

'No.'

Thank fuck for that.

'But I will tell you something...'

Don't look at Cross. Don't look at Cross. Don't look

'Whatever's going on, it's serious...'

Jack looked at Cross.

Bollocks.

'How do you mean?'

'After the presser, just before I phoned you earlier, I got a phone call. My editor. He never calls at this time of night.'

Cross asked, 'What did he say?'

Damien paused for a second and Jack got the image of him checking over his shoulders before he spoke. 'He told me to leave this story alone. To come in tomorrow, he had something really good for me...'

Jack and Cross both swigged at their whiskeys.

'He's never got anything good for me. He fucking hates

me. But that's not all...'

The two men lowered their glasses, as if their moves were choreographed.

'I've spoken to another couple of the guys from other papers. They've been warned off it too.'

Jack stood up and rounded his desk, raising his eyebrows at Cross. 'Okay, Damien. Thanks for that. Probably best if we don't speak for a while then, eh.'

'I'd say so.'

They ended the call.

'Curiouser and curiouser...' Cross said, draining his glass.

Jack glanced at the clock. It was half past one in the morning. They'd been at the airport for 12 hours.

'Another?' said Jack, draining his own glass and getting ready to pour.

'When in Rome,' Cross said standing and taking his glass for a top-up.

'Don't.'

'What?' Cross replied, his tone suggesting he knew exactly what Jack was talking about.

'Don't say it.'

'I wasn't going to say anything.'

'You were going to say how odd it all is and that none of it makes sense and that there was once a case of a UFO.'

'I was going to say nothing of the sort!'

'Well?'

'What?'

'Go on. Let's hear it.' Jack said looking around.

Cross took his glass and returned to the settee, 'I shan't give you the pleasure…'

Jack smiled and poured his own drink.

'It is odd though, isn't it?'

Jack turned and had a swig of whiskey. He might need a few of these tonight. 'Okay, tell me this. In all your UFO stories, how many planes have come back?'

Cross smiled. 'I thought you'd never ask.'

10

'And you think that's what's happened here?' Jack asked.

'Why rule it out? That's all I'm saying.'

'Because it's mental?' Jack was having a hard time with this. 'Flights returning late and the pilots reporting strange lights… I mean… this thing was gone for days, Danny. *Days*.' He trusted Cross, but…

But…

There it was. He barely knew Daniel Cross. He knew he was an occult specialist – a Doctor of Parapsychology - who helped the police when their cases took a turn for the weird. An author. A lecturer. He'd lost a son to cancer when the boy was five, and that the loss of the boy brought about the end of his marriage. Despite his unassuming appearance, Cross was undoubtedly a brave man, willing to risk everything to get to the truth, their work together on the Laszlo Breyer case had proven as much. Yet still there was a nagging doubt. Jack

Talbot trusted Cross enough to let him sleep at his house, but...

That word again. From the previous case they'd worked together and since his arrival here, Jack had the impression that Cross knew more than he was letting on. More than that, he knew more than he had a right to. Back in York he'd got the feeling that Cross was able to intuit his thoughts.

'You're struggling with it,' Cross said.

'I just think there are other things we need to rule out before we start looking toward the supernatural, that's all.'

Cross put his glass down, 'Is it?'

'What?'

'All. Is it "all?" You look like you want to ask me something.'

Jack wrestled with the craziness of the idea for a second. Normally he'd never hold anything back. So why wasn't he asking this question?

Because you're afraid. For the first time you're afraid. Afraid of the answer.

'Fuck it,' Jack said, a tone of "here goes" in his voice. 'Can you see the future?'

'Wow. Er... I don't know what to say.'

'Look I'm not being funny, but... You come down here, and, of all the weekends you might have visited your old buddy Jack, this all kicks off. Did you have... an inkling?'

Cross raised his glass again and took a swig. He nodded. 'An inkling. Yes. I suppose I did.'

Jack stood. 'Jesus.'

'It's not as weird as it sounds.'

'Look,' Jack started, 'let's, just for a second, pretend I'm not a bit hurt that you'd use me as an excuse to further your research—'

'Jack,' Cross said pleadingly.

Jack wasn't listening. 'Did you know she'd come back?'

'Hannah? No. Never. It doesn't work like that.'

'So how does it work? Because I'm not going to lie, it sounds fucking weird.'

'Have you ever had déjà vu?'

'Who hasn't?'

'You'd be surprised.'

Jack remembered Cross had told him that not everyone experienced déjà vu before. The thought made him squirm and took the edge off his frustration.

'That's the same?'

'To a certain extent, yes. I suppose mine's more developed. I'll get a feeling - an inkling - and by focusing on it, yes, I can get certain intuitions.'

'That sounds *weird*.'

'You're a detective,' Cross said.

Jack shrugged.

'You've never had a hunch?'

'Well, yeah, but—'

'How would you describe that to someone who had no idea what a hunch was? Wouldn't they say it was weird?'

'I suppose.'

'You ever solved a case with nothing other than a hunch?'

'I need evidence. *Proof*. That's why I can't accept stories about UFOs.'

'That's fair enough. I'm not asking you to buy into it heart and soul. I just think we should keep an open mind.'

'By "we" you mean—'

He smiled. 'You.'

Jack smiled too. He drained his glass. 'I think I've had enough for one night.'

'Yeah,' Cross sighed as he polished off the remains of his glass. 'Till tomorrow?'

Jack looked at Cross. 'I'm still hurt...'

'Jack.'

Jack turned and left. 'And it's still weird.'

'Night, Jack,' Cross shouted.

Jack shouted back, 'Very weird.'

CHAPTER FOUR

THE NEXT MORNING Jack and Cross sat in Ruth Draper's living room. Since Ruth had been in the kitchen making tea, Jack had been surveying the surroundings, trying to get more of an idea of who Ruth Draper was. There wasn't much to go on. The house was warm and inviting enough, clean, tidy, but the furnishings were sparse. Something that fit with Ruth's cold personality. One thing that didn't fit were the photos of twin girls - barely seven years old. There were no toys anywhere that Jack could see, even though they'd only seen the living room.

Ruth Draper entered carrying a tray.

'Nice photos,' Jack said as she lay the tray on the table.

Ruth looked round, 'Ah, yes, the girls. They've been staying with their dad. They wanted to come round and see auntie Hannah, but she's not quite up to it yet.'

Jack and Cross reached for their cups as Ruth sat in an armchair. She didn't appear as tired, and although that empty uncertainty at her sister's whereabouts was gone from her eyes, she still looked troubled.

'How is Hannah doing?' Cross asked.

Ruth sighed a little. 'She's tired. Confused. She doesn't quite seem herself. I didn't want to press her into discussing what had happened.'

'That's probably wise. She'll need time,' Cross said.

'It was weird though,' Ruth said. 'It came on the news, the hijacking story, and I went to turn it off, you know, to avoid triggering anything, but she barely reacted. She asked me what I was doing, like I'd gone mad.'

'What did you do?' Jack said.

'I left it on. They mentioned the hijacking, says she can't remember it.'

'Any of it?' Cross said.

'Not a thing.'

'Is that normal?' Jack asked Cross.

'Any traumatic event like this, it might happen that the event itself is removed from the conscious memory and stored in the subconscious, to protect the individual from the trauma itself.'

'But the whole thing?' Jack glanced at Ruth and saw her concern in his disbelief, cleared his throat and switched his focus back to Cross.

'For something like this, it is unusual that the entire event can't be recalled.'

Ruth lowered her voice to just above a whisper, 'I must say, she didn't seem disturbed by what had happened. There was a frustration at not being able to remember anything. Like she wanted to recall it, but simply couldn't. And she kept repeating that none of what she was saying was to leave the house. She was very certain on that.'

Jack raised his hands to gesture that his silence was guaranteed.

THE VANISHING OF FLIGHT 187

'Have you been in touch with the Lutton girl?'

'Nicola? No. I never thought to be honest. We got back so late...' The idea tailed off into a moment of deep thought.

Jack pulled out his notepad and scribbled a reminder that that would be a line of enquiry worth pursuing.

Ruth sighed again, 'I thought this would all be over when she got home. How naive of me.'

'Things will get back to normal, it will just take time,' Jack said, Daniel Cross nodding along with the sentiment.

'I don't want to sound cold; Hannah means the world to me...'

That much was obvious. Jack couldn't recall a big sister so protective.

'But time is not really something I have. Work's piling up and Julian, the girl's dad, is getting impatient. He loves having the girls, but...' Again, she tailed off, the frustration visible.

Cross glanced at Jack, then at Ruth, 'There is one thing we could do... to speed things up.'

Jack turned to Cross and Ruth looked up, hopefully.

'Obviously, Hannah would have to agree to it, but if she's as frustrated as you say she is at her memory loss, she might go for it...'

'What did you have in mind?' Ruth asked.

Even though Jack had no idea Cross possessed such skills, he knew what was coming next.

Cross cleared his throat, 'I could hypnotise her.'

'I'll do it.'

The voice came from behind Jack. He turned to see a

figure standing in the doorway. It was Hannah.

2

Jack, Cross and Ruth sat round Hannah in the living room, and only now Hannah was with them did Jack feel the shift in atmosphere. It was odd before, like being in a house still in the gentle hold of a recent bereavement. Now that Hannah was there with them, it had changed. It almost felt like the direct aftermath. That heaviness when you've had to break the bad news in person. It struck Jack as very odd, as no one had died, but the feeling was there all the same.

'Okay,' Jack said to Hannah, 'before we decide whether or not to go ahead with the hypnosis, we just need to ask Nicola what she can remember.'

Cross took over. 'The odds of the both of you being unable to remember a single moment of the same event are extremely high. Hopefully, your friend will recall something. Even the tiniest detail could trigger something for you.'

Jack placed a hand gently on her shoulder, 'Are you sure you're okay with this?'

Hannah just nodded, picked up the mobile phone, and dialled. She engaged the loudspeaker and set the ringing phone back on the table. After a few rings, Nicola answered.

'Hi Nix, just thought I'd call and see how you're doing.'

There was a pause before Nicola spoke.

'I'm okay. Are you...? Are you alone?'

Hannah locked eyes with Jack as she spoke. 'Yeah. Why?'

'Just... you know.'

Jack felt Cross's eyes him, the odd response already noted.

'Listen, Nix, I wanted to ask you something... The whole flight thing. The hijacking. I... I can't remember any of it.'

'That's a good thing, right?' Nicola's response was faster this time.

'Is it? Not a single thing. No hijackers, no guns, no knives, no demands. Nothing.'

'I'm not sure I want to remember.'

Hannah looked back up at Jack. He gestured that she was doing well and for her to keep going.

'Don't you think it's weird? What can you remember?'

Again, silence fell at the other end of the line. Ruth now looked at Jack.

'Nix?' Hannah pressed her friend. 'Are you there?'

After another pause Nicola replied. Her voice sounded like what she was saying was coming to her as a complete revelation.

'Nothing. I can't remember anything.'

Jack scribbled on his notepad and showed it to Hannah. She read it and nodded.

'Oh well,' she said, 'I'm sure it's nothing to worry about. It'll come back in time... Listen, I should go, Ruth's made breakfast. Call me if you need anything. Love you.'

The phone call ended, and Jack and Cross exchanged a look as Ruth comforted Hannah.

'Danny, can I speak to you outside for a moment?'

Jack and Cross faced off on Ruth Draper's lawn and spoke in hushed tones.

'How safe is this?' Jack asked, hands on hips. 'You said her subconscious was protecting her.'

Cross held his hands out, 'It's not one-hundred percent, but it might be our only hope of getting to the bottom of what really happened.'

Jack was already shaking his head, 'Not if it puts Hannah at risk.'

'Of course. That's the last thing I want, but I can't give you a stonewall guarantee.'

Jack stared off into the distance, turning his wedding ring on his finger. 'I'm not sure about this.'

Cross stepped forward, 'Hannah wants to know what happened to her more than anyone, the final choice should be hers.'

Jack knew Cross was right, of course the final decision lay with Hannah, which he felt was something Ruth wouldn't be too happy about, but this could be the only way to confirm what happened. Ruth gets the proof she needs, Hannah and Cross get their answers, and he gets paid. But it still made him uncomfortable.

'We've tried everything else. Don't you find it odd that Nicola can't recall a single thing, the same way Hannah can't?'

Had they tried everything else? Cross was right; the fact that neither of them remembered anything was very odd. A statistical anomaly. The staff at the airport had led to dead ends, although David's promise that his colleague in the tower would contact them was still to come to fruition.

'I just want to be sure we've exhausted every other avenue. I could lean on David again. His colleague from the tower was supposed to get back to us.'

Cross paced a few steps before turning back. 'You're right, but you saw him. He was scared.'

He was. And he didn't come across as the type to scare easily. His reactions all the way along were as if he felt his job was at risk. Jack's mind went back to the rainy night at the industrial estate and the car that followed him from David's place. Maybe he was afraid of more than losing his job. Which left him waiting for the Freedom of Information requests coming back. And Hannah.

Jack rubbed his forehead, then looked up at Cross. 'Give me the worst case-scenario.'

3

Jack stood behind Cross, hands in pockets, the thumb on his left hand playing with his wedding ring. He'd noticed that since they'd started to discuss the possibility of hypnosis, Ruth's hand had gone to her necklace, fiddling constantly at the fine chain. Cross was sitting on the armchair, body angled directly at Hannah.

'Hannah, what we would be doing is hypnotic regression. I'll take you back through the events of that day, starting with the morning, working through the afternoon, things that your conscious mind has no problem recalling. Then we'll get to the evening. The airport, boarding the flight, and then the missing time. Your mind has the information you're looking for, all of it. The memory is stored in your subconscious. The likelihood is, it's there because it's protecting you.'

'From what?'

'That's what we'll find out. It might be unpleasant, and once it's out, that is something we'll have to deal with.'

'How safe is this?'

Ruth was staring at Cross, motionless but for that constant fidgeting with her necklace.

He looked up at her. 'The way the subconscious works, the information stored there could be revealed at any time. For example, if there was a hostage situation—'

'There wasn't.'

They all turned to Hannah.

'I know that's what they said on the news, but it's wrong. I'd be able to remember that. Nix certainly would.'

Silence followed. After a couple of seconds, Cross broke it.

'Just as an example, if there *was* a hostage situation, a scene in a film could trigger the memory. A car-backfiring might remind you of gunfire. Whatever happened, the memory could be triggered at any time. Here, we'll have more control over it.'

'I'll do it,' Hannah said. Her words held more conviction than anything Cross or Jack had ever heard her say. In that moment, the fog had lifted from her eyes and the confused young woman had gone. 'On one condition.'

Jack replied. 'Go ahead.'

'Whatever we uncover, however big or small, it stays in this room.'

'Of course,' Jack said.

Cross cleared his throat, 'I, er... would like to record the session. Just for my personal notes.'

Hannah nodded. 'As long as you don't show it to anyone, that's fine.'

Ruth stepped closer to her sister. 'Hannah, the airline are hiding something and with this information I could take them to court—'

Hannah's whole body tensed. 'No.'

Everyone instinctively moved back. For the first time since the return, Hannah showed raw emotion. She had almost screamed the word. She drew a deep breath and composed herself.

'You have to promise that whatever comes out through this does not leave this room. All of you. Or I won't do it.'

Jack replied. 'That's absolutely fine with me. Listen, Hannah, if you don't want to—'

'I do,' she said, that conviction back in her eyes. 'But that's the condition.'

Cross nodded. 'Okay.'

Hannah looked up at Ruth. 'Sis?'

Ruth said nothing. Just nodded twice in quick, short movements. And that was that. Hannah Draper would undergo hypnosis.

4

'Okay Hannah, where are you?'

Cross was focused totally on the young Draper sister. Ruth sat across from her, recording the whole event on a mobile phone.

Hannah's face was serene calm in the dim shade of the room.

'I'm at my place.'

'Good,' said Cross, his tone soothing. 'Tell me what you see.'

Jack watched on, notepad on knee, awaiting anything that could help solve the riddle of what really happened on Flight 187. Cross had told him outside that they might have to do this a few times. That there might not be anything concrete that came from the first session, just hints at the truth. Someone should tell that to his sweaty palms.

Hannah replied to Cross in cool monotone. 'My suitcase is on my bed. I'm packing for my trip, trying to figure out what I don't need.'

'What you don't need?'

'I can't fit everything in. Ruth's upset.'

'Ruth is there?'

'She's in the living room. She's saying I need to hurry up and that I'm always late. That I've already packed once for the cancelled flight. She doesn't understand how I'm not ready.'

Jack turned to Ruth to verify if that really happened. Ruth nodded.

THE VANISHING OF FLIGHT 187

'Okay,' Cross said, 'moving forward in time now, you've left your house, where are you now?'

Hannah's gentle features darkened with a frown. 'We're in the car. On the way to pick Nix up. Ruth's pissed off. The traffic is bad. She says it's my fault for taking so long.'

'This is good Hannah, what else can you tell me?'

'The radio is on. But it's not playing anything good. Ruth listens to rubbish.' Hannah smiled softly. 'We're at Nic's place now. She's on the doorstep, ready to go. She looks like she's been waiting a while. She's never late.'

Cross and Jack both looked at Ruth now. The baseline test was over, they just had to see if she'd passed. Ruth nodded. Her recollections of the day up to the flight matched with those of her sister.

'Very good, Hannah, so let's move to the airport. What's happening?'

'The building is brightly lit. We're late. We're following Ruth. She always knows what to do. She's asking us if we've got our boarding cards and passports ready. We're really late.' She bit her bottom lip. 'I'm worried.'

'Because you're late?'

'Because of the storm.'

One of the early theories about the plane was that it had been hit by lightning. That fit in with the weather reports.

'Okay good. Then what?'

'We check our suitcases and say goodbye to Ruth, and she says she'll pick us up when we get back. There's a queue at security but our names are mentioned over the announcements and we go straight to the front. There are no problems and we go to the gate. A lady checks our boarding passes. Her hair is really nice, long like Nic's, but she's wearing too much makeup.'

Jack tapped the end of is pencil against the blank sheet of notepad. Cross glanced over. He stopped.

'Okay so now where are you?'

'We're on the plane. People look angry with us. They're all in their seats and we've just got on. We take our seats and the attendants put our bags in the overhead compartments for us. Then we take off.'

'Do you notice anything unusual?'

Hannah frowned again. A tiny gesture, but Jack leaned forward in anticipation.

'No.'

Jack leaned back.

'It's a normal take off. Very smooth. Even Nix said so. I don't know if she's just saying it for me. She knows I don't like flying. Nix is looking out of the window. The clouds are lit up. I only glance. Nix is glued to it. She's in the window seat. I'm in the aisle seat reading the magazine. Well, flicking through it. Then the fasten seatbelts light goes off. An attendant arrives. Her nails are really nice. We buy drinks—'

'What drinks?'

'Vodka. With coke.'

'Okay, and...'

Hannah's forehead wrinkled. 'The fasten seatbelts light is back on. The pilot is warning everyone to take their seats.'

THE VANISHING OF FLIGHT 187

'Do the attendants sit?'

Cross was trying to get an idea of how bad it was. Jack scribbled on his pad.

'No. The attendant seems fine. Then...' She swallowed. 'The plane is shuddering. Nix looks frightened.'

'Are you afraid?'

'Yes. The attendant looks nervous. Then there's a loud bang.'

A bang. It couldn't have been a bomb. After all, the flight made it back okay. Everyone was leaning closer to Hannah now and Jack realised he was holding his breath.

'It's turbulence and it was quite bad, but the attendant smiles, so I feel relaxed. I'm squeezing the life out of the armrests. I wish Nix was sitting next to me.'

'Very good Hannah then what?'

Hannah's chest rose and fell rapidly now. 'There's a bright flash—'

'What kind of flash?'

'It lights the whole inside of the plane up like daylight. Broad daylight.'

'It's inside the plane?'

A flashbang grenade? Used to disorient in combat. Something that hijackers might use...

But Hannah was shaking her head.

'No. Not in the plane. It was bright enough to light the whole inside of the plane, but... it looked like it came from outside.'

Jack looked at Cross. Cross raised his eyebrows before

continuing.

'Can you see anything outside?'

'No. It's over now. The turbulence has stopped. Everyone is looking round at each other. People are murmuring.'

'Why?'

'Something's different.'

'What's different, Hannah?'

'I don't know. The sky. It looks... It's daytime.'

Jack scribbled on his pad that the plane had reappeared earlier than when it had gone missing. He showed it to Cross, who gestured that the idea was plausible with a tilt of his head.

'Okay Hannah. What's happening now?'

'The pilot is saying that we're going back to the airport. It's nothing to worry about, but they've been directed to return. Everyone is murmuring. Nix looks scared. She shows me her phone. The battery is dead, so I check mine. Mine is dead too. People are confused. Some have their voices raised. The attendants are calming everyone down.'

'What do you see now?'

'We're landing. Back at the airport. Something is going on; you can tell by the attendants. They're acting weird.'

'Weird how?'

'Like they know something. They're keeping it a secret. The plane has landed, and some people are standing up. Before the seatbelts light's gone off. The attendants are telling them to sit down. And then—'

Her faced darkened again. Her breathing was short, and

she gripped the cushion of the sofa beneath her.

Cross was leaning forward now. 'What is it Hannah? What do you see?'

'Men are getting on.' She swallowed hard. 'They've got guns.'

5

Guns. The mention of guns brought the room to momentary silence. Glances were exchanged in all directions and before the idea could fully land that the hijacking story was true, Cross asked his next question.

'The men with guns, Hannah, what do they want?'

Hannah's breathing became short and shallow, clearly affected by the appearance of armed men. 'They've been let onto the plane by the attendants.'

Instead of becoming clearer, the waters were being muddied by the second.

'Why? Did they threaten the crew?'

'No. I don't think so. They weren't there one minute and the next, about fifteen men all armed with machine guns appeared.'

'Fifteen?'

'Yes. There's loads of them.'

'What are they doing now?'

'They're pointing their guns at anyone who makes a noise. Taking mobile phones from people trying to use them. Outside is all blue flashing lights.'

'Are the armed men police?'

'No. I don't think so. They're in some sort of protective clothing. A bit like soldiers. Or riot police. There's an announcement. It's the pilot.'

'What is he saying, Hannah?'

'No, it's not the pilot. But it's over the speakers. A man. Telling us to keep still. That we'll be let go soon. But we need to answer some questions. We'll be taken off the plane in small groups, and then we can go. A man is standing up. Saying that they can't keep us here. He's saying that his phone said it's not Thursday it's Sunday. And someone else agrees. One of the men is telling him to keep quiet. Points his gun right in his face. Passengers are murmuring.'

'What do you see?'

'The man with the gun… he's smashed the passenger in the face. People are screaming. The men with guns are now pointing them at the rest of us. To quiet us down. Nobody is talking at all now. The plane is moving again.'

'Where to? What can you see out of the windows?'

'The flashing lights are there. Police. I can see the stairs being taken away. We're moving… into a big building.'

'Like a hangar?'

'Yes.'

At Ruth's house, the sky had darkened behind the curtain and gentle rain tapped against the window. Hannah had been under for thirty minutes and already Jack had questions to ask.

THE VANISHING OF FLIGHT 187

'What's happening now?'

Cross had been asking the same question over and over, but he didn't seem bored. On the contrary, each time he asked revealed some new if incomplete information that would have remained covered otherwise.

'They're taking some people off the plane. The left side. The front half.'

Jack knew from the passenger list that it meant roughly forty people had got off. Where were they going?

'Some people are complaining,' Hannah said. 'But the gunmen they threaten them. Food and water is being brought aboard while we wait for our turn to get off. It's taking too long. Nix is holding my hand. By the time we get off the plane, it's already dark outside.'

'Are you in the hangar now?'

'Yes. There are more men with guns. They stop us talking to each other, just like on the plane. We're in a sort of separated area. A sheet has been put up like a long curtain around a hospital bed and we've got these uncomfortable chairs. A man is approaching. He asks Nix to follow him. She looks scared. I don't know if I'll see her again. I can hear her shoes as she walks away. She's walking a long way, maybe to the other end of the hangar, until I can't hear her anymore. I don't like it. There's only four of us left. I can tell they're as scared as I am.'

Cross spoke in a cool, soothing voice. 'It's okay, Hannah, I'm right here with you. We can stop this at any time. Are you okay to continue?'

'Yes. There's a man. Walking towards me.'

'Can you describe him?'

'He's normal looking. Plain. I wouldn't know him if I saw him again. He's in a suit. Like a business suit. Black. He wants me to follow him. I'm nervous.'

Jack saw that her leg was trembling, but it felt like they were finally getting somewhere, and that the truth was just around the corner. But Ruth wasn't happy. She was getting jittery, and she looked like she wanted to call the whole thing off. But Hannah kept talking.

'I'm following the man. He walks quickly. Around the curtain, I can see a room at the other end, like an office. We're going there. We are at the door. He asks me to go in and sit down. He's opening the door.'

'What's inside?'

'It's dark. There's a table and one chair. Over the table is a light. But it's only lighting the table, the rest of the room is dark. I can't see anything else. Except on the table, there's two envelopes. Plain brown. When I get nearer I can see my name on them.'

'Do you sit down?'

'Yes. When I do, the room gets darker. The man in the suit has closed the door behind me.'

'Is he in the room?'

'No. I can hear his feet walking away.' Hannah frowned. 'But someone's in here with me.'

'What does he look like?'

Hannah's voice rose in alarm. 'He's behind me. I can't see him. He's telling me to look forward. I'm frightened.'

THE VANISHING OF FLIGHT 187

Jack's biggest worry now was Ruth. She wanted to stop, but they were getting so far. Jack wanted Cross to hurry up before big sister stepped in. Cross sensed what Jack had and carried on; voice hurried by urgency.

'It's okay you're doing well. What is he saying?'

'That the plane was hijacked. That I can't talk about it. To anybody. If they ask, I have to say I don't want to talk about it... He says I have a choice to make.'

Cross waited, knowing she'd go on. Jack knew they didn't have long. Ruth's knee had started bouncing and Jack had lost count of the number of times she'd dried her palms on her clothes. After what was only a few seconds but felt like a lifetime, Hannah spoke.

'He tells me to look in the first envelope.'

Cross looked at Jack before turning back to Hannah. 'What's in there?'

'Wow,' her eyebrows raised. 'It's money.'

'How much?'

'It's not cash. But it says I get money. Half my salary. Every month. Forever. Starting in six months. He says after the furore has died down; I'll get paid, if I keep quiet... but there's a condition...'

Hannah frowned.

'He tells me to open the second envelope.'

'What's inside, Hannah?'

'Oh my God.'

The words were almost screamed, and Hannah squirmed.

'It's pictures. Photographs. It's photos of Ruth. The girls.'

Jack looked at Ruth's in time to see her face blanch.

'He asks me if I understand what the photos are. I understand. It's a threat. I'm angry. I turn around.'

'What do you see?'

'I see his face.' Hannah started crying. 'He's got a gun.'

She was screaming.

Ruth stood up. 'Stop this right now!'

'What does he look like?' Jack asked.

'I can't see! I can't see!'

Her legs were kicking in panic and tears streamed down her face.

'Wake her up!' Ruth screamed.

6

Jack, Cross, Ruth and Hannah all sat around the coffee table, circled around the china tea set like it was some sort of ceremony or ritual. Maybe it was. Hannah's hands still trembled, and Ruth's face was still as white as the cup she drank from. Hannah's reluctance to share anything was now understood, as was Nicola's.

Cross looked at Hannah, 'You did really well, Hannah, that was great...'

Hannah nodded.

'...but,' Cross went on, 'There's still a lot of time missing, and I think if we tried again, we could find out exactly what happened.'

Cross wanted to get to that flash of light. That could be his Holy Grail. Cross had stressed to Jack in their emails that UFO did not mean alien. Unidentified Flying Object. But what if it was that? What if he had evidence, confirmation of life from another world? But Ruth wouldn't allow another hypnosis session, let alone Hannah.

Hannah looked up. 'Okay.'

The room fell into stunned silence.

'Hannah...' Ruth said, her tone one of deep scepticism.

'No, sis. I want to know. I'll do it... But not today. I'm tired. I'd like to lie down.'

Her voice had that same robotic quality that it had before. Empty. Lights on, nobody home. It was only when under hypnosis and distressed she showed any emotion at all.

Hannah stood and the room rose with her. Jack and Cross rose out of courtesy, Ruth to steady her sister and lead her to her room. The moment they were gone, both men sat again looking at each other.

'What is going on here?' Jack asked. 'They wouldn't be officially debriefed because the plane was hit by lightning.'

'My theory doesn't quite sound so mad now, does it?' Cross said without a hint of glee.

Jack could only shake his head.

'Have you ever heard anything like this? Honestly?'

'No.'

Cross looked up at Ruth as she re-entered the room. She entered slowly, unsteady on her feet herself, dropping heavily onto the settee. Jack could see Ruth's thirst for answers had dried up. It was a common occurrence in his line of work. His clients wanted the truth, until it became too much to bear. The truth could be a warm and comforting ally, but it was often a merciless foe. When it was revealed, the lid never went back on the box.

It was a minute before anyone spoke.

'What would you like us to do?' Jack asked.

He hoped the answer came back to keep digging, however unlikely that response was.

'I think I need a bit of time. Can we leave it there for today? Come back tomorrow; when I've had time to sleep on it.'

Jack rose, 'Of course. Danny?'

Cross looked round. 'Oh,' was all he said, like Jack had snapped him from some contemplation. He stood, unsteady on his feet himself.

Ruth closed the door behind them without a word and they trailed back to Jack's car. The rain was still falling in gentle drops, and the sky was now a leaden grey. Jack found that he couldn't look at it, keeping his eyes glued to the path.

As soon as both men were inside the car, Jack spoke.

'What the fuck is this?'

'This could be it, Jack. This might be the proof you wanted.'

The lid doesn't go back on the box.

'Do you think she'll carry on? Ruth, I mean.'

'Honestly, I've no idea. We'll go over what we've got at

the flat and see where we want to go with this,' Jack said, starting the engine. 'Because whatever Ruth Draper wants to do, I want answers.'

7

The question had been gnawing at Jack for too long. He'd broached the subject after a few glasses of whiskey the other night, and sort of written it off as a joke, but outside of all of the questions about the bizarre case of Flight 187, the flight that vanished into thin air for three days before miraculously returning, there was actually another question eating away at him, and he'd held his tongue for long enough.

'Why did you choose this weekend?'

Cross was looking out of the car window, watching the rows of houses in the litter strewn street as they passed by. 'Hmm?'

'I was wondering, what was it that made you decide to visit this week. We've been on about it for a while and then all of a sudden, out of the blue, it has to be this week, and wouldn't you know it, a plane vanishes into thin air and then comes back like a David Copperfield trick.'

For a split-second Jack saw the idea of making an excuse pass through Cross's mind before he ditched the idea completely. Jack may not have had the skills of Daniel Cross, but he was keen enough to know when he was being led down the proverbial path.

'Okay, okay,' Cross said. 'I admit. I had an idea that

something would happen...'

Jack shook his head.

'...but I didn't know what it would be. I just thought... you know, kill two birds with one stone. Squeeze a visit to you in, and while I'm here, get into a little adventure. What could it hurt...'

'Well,' Jack started. 'I've got to say, I feel... used.'

'Jack...' that perish-the-thought tone. 'I can see how it looks, but...'

'I don't know who I'm more pissed off at, you for taking liberties, or me for whining about it like a teenage girl. I just thought... you know... we were mates.'

Jack eyed the crossing before flying through. He just wanted to get home.

Cross turned to Jack. 'Is that what you think? That we're not friends?'

'Well this cheapens the whole... I mean... Oh, fuck it.'

Cross shuffled uncomfortably. 'Well, that was not my intention. I feel like an idiot now. I never even thought...'

'Didn't see *that* coming, did you?'

The silence was uncomfortable for the first time since Cross had visited.

'Well, fuck it, you're here now,' Jack said, 'So what do you reckon?'

'About?'

'The flight?'

Cross shrugged, 'It's clear now why David was so reluctant to talk. It wouldn't surprise me if there has been

THE VANISHING OF FLIGHT 187

some sort of pressure put on the airport employees to keep quiet. Perhaps not to the extent that Hannah experienced, that was a threat, pure and simple.'

Jack nodded. He felt bad for adding to David's pressure by hounding him for info, even if that was the only point he had to squeeze at the time.

Cross went on, 'I don't mean to blow my own trumpet with the UFO theory, but what Hannah described does sound eerily similar to some other cases I've heard of. But I've never been this close myself...'

Jack let the UFO comment slide. He didn't feel like getting into that discussion now. He was still reeling from the idea that Cross had somehow used him. It wasn't the using that bothered him, but rather the feeling of hurt he got from it. Feelings like that don't happen to middle aged men. It had been an emotional few days, that was all. He hoped.

They arrived back at the flat and it was still only the afternoon. Jack anticipated another one of those days of waiting. Watching time ebbing away as the case sat in limbo, not regressing, not moving forward, but instead stuck in time while the next development broke. This case had reached the point where the next development hinged on whether Hannah Draper's curiosity was greater than her fears. In cases like this, curiosity could be deadly.

The evening hours were spent in a strange mood, Jack annoyed and distracted by his hurt feelings, Cross overcompensating with niceties at his mistake. They speculated over the missing time Hannah had experienced before drunken storytelling took over. But the clumsy awkwardness was still there, and after a short time, Jack excused himself and went to bed. Tomorrow, he hoped, they'd get another run at Hannah.

If not, this case was dead in the water.

8

They awoke early, had a light breakfast, and headed straight to see Ruth. The usual excited chatter and speculation absent, that odd feeling still weighing heavy on the mood. Jack was disappointed. Hurt even. When he thought about it, he didn't have any friends. He and Tommy had barely spoken since the Breyer case, even though his ex-partner (and ex-brother-in-law) had said he could count on him. The reality was, they had exchanged a couple of phone calls and nothing more. While Jack usually found it easy to make friends, he was alone down here - one of the reasons he'd been so looking forward to Cross's visit. The closest thing Jack had to a friend apart from Cross was Damien, and that was more of a business arrangement. They'd never met outside of exchanging info on cases, which was a pity. Jack liked Damien and thought that they could be friends, if things were different.

Jack pulled up at Ruth's house, hoping that Hannah was in the mood to talk.

'Well,' Cross sighed, 'shall we?'

Cross's tone was heavy, like he knew if nothing happened here, he'd end up going back to York, and that would be it. That was how Jack saw things, at least.

THE VANISHING OF FLIGHT 187

Jack eyed the house, like it was an adversary, and without taking his eyes from it, said, 'Let's go.'

They made their way along the path, not striding like men on a mission, but shuffling like men awaiting execution.

Jack knocked. A car went by and both he and Cross watched suspiciously as it passed. They turned back to the house and Jack held out a hand. His head tilted as he listened, and Cross did the same.

From inside the house, Jack heard shouting.

'Ruth?' Cross whispered.

It was unclear which of the Draper sisters it was. He knocked again. This time, after a few seconds, a shape appeared at the other side of the frosted glass. The door opened. It was Ruth.

'Who the fuck is it?' a frustrated voice shouted from inside.

Ruth's face flushed red. Her eyes were dull and ringed in dark circles. Whatever was going on now looked like it had been going on most of the night. 'It's not a good time.'

'We can come back...' Jack offered.

But Ruth was already shaking her head. 'I don't think that will be—'

'I said, who the fuck's there?' Hannah's voice was now a shriek, touched by an unhinged quality that made Jack long for the dull monotone of the previous afternoon.

'It's nobody. I'll be there in a minute, Hannah,' Ruth shouted back into the house. 'I should be going. I'll pay you in full, as we agreed—'

'No,' Jack said, 'that won't be necessary—'

'As we agreed.' Ruth finished. 'Now, please. I must go.'

Without another word, Ruth Draper shut the door, instantly turning and speaking loudly to sooth her sister. Jack and Cross were left with no choice. They about turned and trudged back to the car. The single lead in the case of Flight 187 was dead. It was over.

9

The sticky air grew heavier outside as storm clouds gathered on the horizon. In the hour since Ruth had shut the door in their faces that was the only thing that had changed. Jack was tired of staring at Ruth's house, and Cross sensed it.

'Well?' he asked.

'Well,' Jack sighed, 'it looks like that's it.'

'Something weird is going on.'

'I don't doubt that for one second,' Jack agreed, 'but until Ruth Draper says she needs us, we're done.'

He started the engine and u-turned back in the direction of home.

Cross wasn't willing to give up quite as easily. 'Did you read the articles I sent you?'

'You did send me a lot...'

Every couple of weeks, Cross would send a story about some unusual phenomena. Jack supposed he was trying some sort of soft conversion to get him to believe in all the mad stuff Cross did. Some of them were interesting, some were crazy. Some was conspiracy stuff about Russian apartment bombings actually being the work of the FSB and not Chechen terrorists (although he had to admit that one was a case that didn't stand up to much scrutiny and warranted much deeper investigation). There was one fascinating theory that posited we're all living in a computer simulation. A ridiculous idea at first, but the more he read the more it became strangely plausible. But Jack's mind quickly went back to driving. He was focused more on the road than on Daniel Cross. The resentment - the hurt - was still there.

'The one about the Japan Airlines incident...' Cross tailed off.

Jack did recall that story. A cargo plane flying over Alaska accompanied by a giant craft. One of the more interesting cases, because the pilot's story was backed up by ground radar.

'Pilots see things while flying all of the time, but they just don't get reported.'

Jack indicated to turn into his street. They were back already.

'That may very well be the case,' Jack said, 'but this case, for now is closed.'

He parked up and they got out, Cross hurrying to keep up with Jack as he went for home.

'Don't you care?' Cross asked.

Jack stopped and turned. 'What difference does it make?'

'We're on the verge of something huge here. We could prove that alien life actually exists.'

'There you go again,' Jack snapped. 'Even if there was a UFO, that doesn't mean it was alien. It's a leap of faith that we can't prove. It could just be some advanced technology we've made that we don't know about.'

A grin appeared on Cross's face. 'So you have been reading the articles I sent...'

Jack turned back to the door, 'Yeah well, Hannah's back home, safe and well. I'm done with this.'

'She didn't sound well to me...'

'Cross. Let it go. It's over.'

'What are you afraid of?'

Jack stopped. Jack Talbot was afraid of nothing...

...usually.

He thought for a second. He thought about why he was pissed off with Cross. Was it because he felt let down? That was a part of it, surely but... to accept that, was to accept that Cross did have some sort of gift. And that meant that the impossible was possible. That the case of Laszlo Breyer wasn't just some bizarre one-off. If that was true, then it meant that it was entirely possible that the answer to this puzzle could be from something not of this world. Jack suddenly preferred the Bermuda Triangle theory. And at least Simulation Theory would be a nice, simple explanation for Laszlo Breyer...

'Look,' he turned around, 'maybe it was aliens who borrowed Flight 187. Maybe it was just a hijacking. The fact is, the case is finished; Ruth doesn't want anything to do with us, and the poor woman is probably scared half to death for the life of her kids, but if she doesn't want help, I can't give it to her. Let's go inside, get your things, and I'll take you to the station.'

Cross stared at Jack, with a look that said he had more to say, but he remained quiet. He just shrugged and followed Jack inside.

Jack entered the living room and saw Cross stuffing the last of his things into his bag.

'Ready?'

'Just about.'

Jack made for the door.

'Wait.'

He stopped and turned.

'Listen, Jack,' Cross said, 'I'm sorry I used the whole plane business as an excuse to come down here. It was "not cool" as the kids say. I did want to visit. I... It was stupid of me.'

Jack shrugged. 'Don't worry about it. Thanks for apologising.'

Jack locked up and headed downstairs.

'You know,' Cross started, 'If you wanted, I could get you set up in business in York. Your money will go further up there, and I can throw a few clients your way.'

Jack smiled. 'That's tempting, but no thanks...'

'Oh,' Cross's shoulders slumped.

Jack smiled. 'Too many werewolves.'

They stepped into the warm noon sun and Jack squinted against it, the thunderheads still building ominously all around now. He got to the car and stopped. He quickly glanced in both directions along the street, but it was empty.

'What is it?' Cross asked.

Jack pointed. Tucked under the windscreen wiper was a slip of paper.

CHAPTER FIVE

THEY'D BEEN INSIDE for less than thirty minutes. It was too early to drink and too hot for tea, but that still left more than enough time for someone to leave a note. The street was empty now, just the few cars whose owners worked nights, or didn't work at all, baking in the summer sun.

Jack snatched the note that fluttered beneath his windscreen wiper and opened it. Jack showed Cross the note. Neat, clear handwriting. A name - Sean - and a mobile phone number.

'Who's Sean?'

Jack was about to reply that he had no idea when his phone rang. He shoved the note into his inside pocket and pulled out his phone, glancing at the screen.

'It's Ruth.'

They were speeding through the empty streets towards Ruth Draper's fancy neighbourhood.

'That's all she said?'

'Just come to her place ASAP.'

'That's it?'

'Wouldn't say more. But it had to be now.'

The car screeched around the corner into Holly Drive

and Ruth was already outside. She stumbled up the drive to meet them as they parked.

Jack leapt out, 'What is it?'

Ruth was on the verge of tears, her eyes looked like she'd seen something she wished she hadn't.

'It's Hannah.'

She's dead. They've got to her. We should never have left this morning.

Cross joined them on Ruth's neat front lawn.

Ruth's eyes were glazed. 'It's Hannah, only... it isn't.'

'I'm not sure I follow,' Jack said.

'The woman in my house. She's not my sister.'

A wave of relief washed over Jack that Hannah was alive, but it was quickly replaced by a feeling Jack found hard to pinpoint. But he understood the glazed expression Ruth had, and that heavy silence that hung in the airport.

Jack put an arm around Ruth and turned her to face the house. 'Let's go inside.'

Jack and Cross sat opposite Ruth in her front room. The atmosphere was different again. No longer under the shroud of bereavement, the energy was now that of threat, of violence. Yesterday felt like Jack had arrived to deliver bad news, this was like he'd been called to a domestic.

'She's asleep.' Ruth took a deep drink from a mug of tea, hands trembling.

'We heard the disturbance when we were here this morning,' Cross said.

Jack considered Ruth. The woman in front of him now

was a far cry from the strong, determined character that had marched into his office and demanded proof of conspiracy a few days before. The threats revealed from Hannah's hypnosis had no doubt shaken her - Jack found them disturbing and he wasn't the target - but now she looked confused as well as frightened.

'What makes you say that it isn't Hannah?'

Ruth shook her head. 'I don't know. It just isn't. She's never acted like this. She's usually so happy and... normal. I didn't know if I should call you after what Hannah... said.' Without saying it aloud, she was referring to the plain envelope of photos. 'But now I feel I can't go to the police.'

Jack placed a comforting hand on Ruth's shoulder. 'In my experience, threats are there to keep the truth hidden. To keep you quiet. As long as this stays between us, I'm confident you'll be safe.'

Ruth looked up, 'So no police?'

Jack thought about Damien and the press being silenced. 'We don't know what we're dealing with or who we can trust. Hannah will calm down. She's been through a lot. She just needs time.'

Ruth shook her head. 'I don't know if I can do it. I need to bring the girls home. Julian, their father, he's been a help, but he's got his own affairs to take care of, and I can't tell him what's going on. Not now.'

Cross took a half-step forward. 'Would you like us to talk to her? Perhaps we can find out why she's acting the way she is.'

Jack nodded. 'It might be a good idea. She might be more

open to sharing with us. She might be trying to protect you.'

Ruth's face brightened a little. 'Would you?'

These were dark waters. Threats had already been made against Ruth, and her children. They were in the middle of a huge cover-up, one that had spread its arms to include keeping the press quiet, if what Damien had said was anything to go by. Jack glanced at Cross, a man whose life had already been endangered in the Breyer case. Cross gave a small shrug. He was willing to put himself at risk to get to the truth, and despite all that had gone on, Jack was willing to do the same to protect him, and the members of the Draper family. But something about this case gave him a bad feeling.

'Of course,' Jack smiled. 'Happy to.'

2

'She seems totally different.' Ruth said in a whisper, making fresh tea.

Hannah had awoken and shuffled into the living room like the half-there zombie she'd been ever since Jack had known her.

'Different how?'

'I mean different from this morning. She was manic. Shouting. Now she seems drugged. There's something wrong.' She stopped stirring the tea in the pot and her eyes filled with tears, 'That's not my Hannah—'

Jack placed a finger to his lips at Ruth's rising tone. 'We'll figure it out. She seems willing to cooperate, let's just see what we can find out. You'll see. It's her, we just need to give her time.'

Back in the living room, Jack positioned himself opposite Hannah, with Cross to the side and Ruth behind. 'I'd like to ask you a few questions Hannah, just to check your memory - no hypnosis. Do you think that would be okay?'

Hannah just nodded.

'Tell me about your childhood. Where did you grow up?'

Hannah smiled a little and started talking. 'Not far from here. Cooper Lane. It's about fifteen minutes away, near the woods. Me, Ruth, mum and dad.'

Her speech was slow and considered, almost like she was concussed, but her eyes smiled, this was a genuine memory.

Jack glanced at Ruth, who nodded.

'You're smiling, Ruth. Was it a happy time?'

'Yes very. I mean, dad worked a lot, but generally things were great. It was a great place to grow up.'

'Did you and Ruth have any hobbies, Hannah?'

Hannah smiled. 'We rode horses. At the weekends. Ruthie was better than me. I preferred swimming.'

Ruth nodded again.

'And did you have any pets?'

'We did. A chocolate Labrador. Benny. And a tortoise, Colin. Ruth named him.'

Jack again looked at Ruth, who again nodded. After a few more questions were met with nods, Jack asked to be excused and took Ruth into the hallway with him. The carpets were thick, and the walls adorned with photos of Ruth, Hannah, and the girls.

'I still don't like it,' Ruth said, again speaking in that rough whisper.

'She's answered anything I've thrown her way. Is there any way she'd know these things if it was not Hannah?'

Ruth stared at the floor and shook her head.

'She's clearly been through a lot. Just give her time.'

'What is it though? What has she been through? There was no hijacking.'

Jack had no reply. He was saved by a shout from the living room.

'Ruth?'

It was Hannah. They re-entered the living room, to find Hannah turned around in her chair to face them.

'What is it, sweetheart?' Ruth asked.

Hannah looked at Cross, then back at her sister. 'Do you want to hypnotise me again?'

3

Just as he had the day before, Cross led Hannah, step by step, through the events of the day leading up to the flight. She recalled things with greater detail drawing them in until Jack felt he could have been on the plane himself. Hannah was under Cross's spell once more, and once more, the room held its breath as they approached the flash of missing time.

'You're doing well, Hannah, really well. Now take your time... what happens after the plane shudders.'

THE VANISHING OF FLIGHT 187

Her face darkened into a frown. 'I'm scared. Nix is too. The fasten seatbelt light comes on. Then... There's a bright flash. From outside. It fills the plane, so it's like daytime. Brighter, even.'

'Good, that's good. Now what do you see?'

'Now it is daytime. Everyone is just sitting in their seats. I look at Nix. People are talking. No one knows what's going on. The pilot makes an announcement. He says we're going back to the airport.'

'Okay, Hannah, I'd like you to try something for me... Imagine what you're seeing is not in your mind, but on a TV screen. A screen you can control. You have a remote control, in fact. You can rewind, fast forward, pause. Can you imagine that?'

'Yes.'

'Good. I'd like you to rewind what you see now, back to the moment of the flash... When you see the flash, I want you to pause. Do you understand?'

Hannah simply nodded.

'Pause, and then freeze frame one frame at a time... Look out of the window Hannah. Describe what you see.'

Hannah's breathing quickened. Her chest rose and fell in short, shallow gasps. A small whine emitted, and her head shook from side to side. 'No. No.'

'What do you see, Hannah? Tell me what you see.'

She gripped the cushions beneath her, her knuckles alabaster white. 'I can't. I can't.'

Ruth's hand went from her necklace to cover her mouth.

'Yes, you can Hannah. It's fine.'

But it wasn't fine. She was shaking her head violently from side to side, rejecting whatever image had appeared on the screen in her mind's eye.

She screamed. 'I can't I can't I can't.'

Her hand made a gesture as if she were pressing a button on a remote control.

'What are you doing Hannah?'

'I don't want to be here.'

'No Hannah, it's fine.' Cross was pleading now. 'Hannah, you're safe, you're in control. Hit pause.'

She froze, motionless.

'Hannah?' Cross said, his wavering voice worrying Jack. 'Hannah, are you okay?'

Hannah was still. Jack's eyes were glued to her chest, the shallow rise and fall, now imperceptible. He was wondering if anyone had ever died under hypnosis.

'Hannah. I want you to tell me what you see.'

Hannah spoke in a voice so quiet, Jack was surprised he heard her at all. 'I'm afraid.'

Cross's body sank in relief. 'Where are you now Hannah?'

'I'm in the hangar,' she whispered.

Cross whispered too, 'What can you see?'

'I've turned around, even though he told me not too... I can see him. I can see his face.'

Jack stood in the hallway with Cross.

'*I'm* freaking out now. Now *I* think it's a fucking UFO.'

Cross smiled gleefully, aware of the huge implications of

THE VANISHING OF FLIGHT 187

such a discovery.

'All right, all right, let's not get ahead of ourselves,' Jack said, trying to temper the excitement.

'But don't you see what this means?'

'It doesn't mean anything yet... What about the man, in the hangar, the interviewer, can you get more info on him?'

Cross nodded, 'I might be able to do better than that.'

'What do you mean?'

'I might be able to get a sketch.'

Jack's eyes widened, 'Like a police sketch?'

Cross smiled and nodded.

'Okay, great, you do that. I'll go and pay Nicola a visit, I want to see if everything's okay over there...'

Jack paused.

'What?' Cross asked.

'This man in the shadows, doing the interviews, putting the frighteners on everyone... do you think...?'

Cross nodded, 'Yes. But there's only one way to find out.'

'Okay, I'll leave it with you. See you back here in an hour?'

Cross nodded. Jack left the house and entered the twilight evening, skies darkened by the clouds that had loomed on the horizon which now blotted out any hint of starlight. Jack couldn't help but look up, unsure whether he hoped to catch sight of something. Anything. But the skies were empty, so far as he could tell. It came as a relief.

'One step at a time, Jacky boy.'

4

The storm had finally arrived as Jack meandered through the rainy streets on the short journey to the home of Nicola Lutton. Hannah's hypnosis testimony ran through his mind. After the bizarre story she'd told, he was halfway convinced that Cross was right, there could be something to the idea of UFOs.

He didn't want it to be true. Above all else, he hoped that whatever greeted him at Nicola's was better than the madness he'd left behind. Then he could write it off as one person handling the stress of a hijacking badly. If all was well with Nic, then he'd be more than happy to tuck Hannah's story in the "nonsense" file and quickly move along.

What did Tommy always say? Wish in one hand and shit in the other, see which fills up first.

One thing he had little doubt about was the sketch that Cross was making now. He'd bet money to mouse shit that came back as the military man they'd seen at the airport.

The Lutton house was in total darkness. He checked his watch. Just after nine. Too early for everyone to be in bed and the other houses had lights on, so it was nothing to do with the storm. The garage being closed meant he couldn't say for sure if they were in or out, but last time, they'd parked their car in the street. *Ready to take off in an emergency.* He wanted to text Cross but was afraid to disturb the session with Hannah. He decided to call Damien.

'Mr Tee,' Damien said in faux cheerfulness.

'Alright, smart arse,' Jack replied, 'just wondered if you'd

THE VANISHING OF FLIGHT 187

heard any more on that case we were talking about.'

'Jesus, Jack,' Damien said, 'you *still* chasing that?'

'Well, it hasn't resolved itself. Why? Have you given up on it?'

Damien chuckled a sour laugh, 'Didn't have a choice. You should see the bollocks my editor is trying to pretend is interesting to move us on from the flight.'

Damien had spoken a few times about going it alone. The "business" wasn't what it was in his old man's day. If it didn't fit a narrative, it didn't go in, no matter how juicy the story. He was waiting to build up his social media following before taking the plunge, but it sounded like Flight 187 had pushed him one step closer to the exit door and a career flying solo.

'Why?' Damien asked, 'Any new developments?'

Lightning exploded in the skies behind Nic's house.

'You wouldn't believe me if I told you,' Jack replied over the heavy drum of rain on the car roof.

Thunder growled and rippled through the skies. 'Try me...' Damien said.

Just at that, a familiar car pulled around the corner.

'It'll have to wait. Got something going on here. We'll have coffee.'

'Sounds delightful.'

Jack hung up. The car coming along the road had Mr Lutton driving, and two people huddled in the back seat, which he could only presume were Nic and her mum. A friendly family outing wouldn't require Nic to be accompanied in the back seat, which meant they'd been somewhere else.

Like a hospital.

'Fucking hell.'

The notion that Hannah's account was nonsense was already starting to crumble.

The car pulled up; dad much too concerned with whatever was going on inside the car to see Jack parked along the road watching his every move. Dad got out and moved to open the door for his daughter as mum dashed around the back of the car. Another bright flash lit up the skies behind the house as a figure rose gingerly from the back seat. The figure was stooped, vulnerable, shrouded in a blanket, shambling up to the front door like an old woman. She shrank against the roar of thunder that shook the streets below.

'Please tell me that's not Nic.'

Dad ushered them inside and glanced both ways before entering the house. Jack surveyed the houses around, and as soon he was sure the neighbour's curtains had stopped twitching, he left the car, jacket over his head, and darted into the downpour.

At the house, lights had come on downstairs, and Jack moved along the garage wall and scaled the fence into the back garden. He froze as the security light came on illuminating sheets of falling rain. One glance inside the house confirmed that the thoughts of all within were far from whatever was occurring in the back garden.

Mrs Lutton led the shrouded figure into a small downstairs room they'd converted into a makeshift bedroom. Jack moved in closer and watched as the two of them sat on the bed, Mrs Lutton comforting the other. Jack could only presume it was Nic, even though he hadn't seen her, blanket still wrapped around and draped over her head. Mrs Lutton said something, rose to her feet and left the room, leaving the shrouded figure alone. Jack watched on as the figure sat motionless, before settling into a gentle rhythmic rocking.

A light came on upstairs, much brighter than the gentle lamplight of Nicola's new room. Jack craned his head upward and traced a route onto the flat roof via a drainpipe where he could get a better view. The storm raged around him as he scaled the flat roof and crept towards the bedroom window. From here he could see the door, and within, Mr Lutton consoling Nic's mother, who was sobbing gently into his neck. Jack moved to the other side, hoping to see just what it was that had so upset Mrs Lutton, but his view was blocked by the angle of the blinds. Then in a moment, Mr Lutton appeared by the window, and Jack froze. If the lightning flashed now, he'd be exposed. It would be easy enough for him to escape, but not something that the Luttons would get over easily, especially as they were already struggling with the unfolding horror in their house. Jack held his breath as the blinds rotated, closing just as a bright flash exploded into the night.

If Jack hadn't seen it with his own eyes, he wouldn't have believed what he saw as those blinds twisted closed. It was clear now what had caused so much dismay for Mrs Lutton. Written on the wall, smeared in two-foot tall letters, were the words

I CAN'T

Jack gagged at the thought of the stench.

While Nic's parents were on clean up, Jack had the chance to see what was going on with Nic. If they'd left her, she'd either calmed down naturally or had been helped along by something given to her at hospital. Thunder boomed and rippled in the clouds overhead as Jack retraced his steps back to the window downstairs. But something was different.

Now the room was in darkness.

Jack crept along the wall, beaten by the warm rain, its smell filling the air. He pressed himself hard against the wall, avoiding the security light sensor until he reached the window. A loose flap of tarpaulin waved in the wind and Jack stopped dead, braced for the burst of security light. His heartbeat was thudding in his ears muffling the constant beat of the rain and he waited, clinging to the wall until he was sure the security light wouldn't leave him exposed. Finally, he turned to the window and peered against the blackness inside. The darkness was a wall. He cupped his hands to the window and leaned in, his breath fogging the glass. The tarp flapped in the wind and he held his breath. But he was safe....then...

An explosion of lightning turned night into day. He was standing nose to nose with Nicola.

Jack fell backwards and screamed. The instant thunder covered his cries and Jack scrambled to his feet. He bolted for the fence and vaulted into the street, sprinting until he reached the car. For two minutes he sat and watched the house, waiting for a reaction. To see if Nic had reacted as he had. But there was nothing.

With a trembling hand, he turned the key in the ignition and set back off for the Draper house. Whatever he'd expected to see at Nicola's house, nothing could have prepared him for the face at that window.

5

'Danny, you didn't see her.'

Jack fought to control the volume of his voice.

'You're sure it was her?'

Jack and Cross were standing in the hallway at Ruth's. As Ruth's immediate family smiled down from the photos on the wall, the woman herself comforted her sister in the next room.

'It was, but she was barely recognisable. Look,' Jack held out a hand, 'I'm still shaking.'

'Christ, Jack, what did you see?'

'It was her, I mean, you've seen the pictures, she's a good-looking girl.'

Cross shrugged, 'Of course.'

'Not anymore.' Jack shook his head, image of Nicola burned into his brain. 'Her hair. Long, blonde, wavy. She's been pulling it out. A lot of it. Just huge clumps missing. And she was bandaged. Her arms. A gauze on her cheek. If I didn't know better, I'd say she's been hurting herself. Scratching herself. And she looks like she hasn't slept a minute since she got back.' Jack thought about the writing smeared on the wall. 'Her mind's gone.'

'How do you—'

'Trust me.'

Cross looked down, and then glanced towards the living room. 'What do we tell Ruth?'

'We don't want to scare her unnecessarily, but she has to know something. We'll just tell her to keep a close eye and that's it's better Hannah isn't left alone.'

'Could we stay?' Cross asked.

'I've thought about it, but while we're in here, we're not out there. Solving this from here is impossible. And I'll need your human lie-detector skills.'

Cross nodded his agreement.

'So,' Jack said, changing the subject, 'the sketch. What have we got?'

Cross's eyes widened, 'I nearly forgot, but wait here... you're not going to believe this.'

Jack raised his eyebrows, 'You'd be surprised.'

Cross reappeared a moment later with the sketch. He turned it around and presented it to Jack. It was the guy from the airport. Mr MI5. The likeness remarkable.

'She started to describe him, and I took a chance. I just drew him as best I could from memory.' Cross swallowed. 'You should have seen her reaction.'

'That's him.'

'So? What next? We're out of leads...'

'Not entirely. What time is it?'

Cross looked at his watch. 'Ten.'

Jack reached to the inside pocket of his jacket and pulled out a slip of paper. The one slid under the wiper of his car

THE VANISHING OF FLIGHT 187

that afternoon. He entered the number into his mobile and dialled.

CHAPTER SIX

THE RELENTLESS RAIN battered the streets as Jack and Cross approached The Star pub. Midweek the place would be half empty, especially this near closing time in such dreadful weather. They were on their way to meet Sean, the owner of the phone number slid under Jack's windscreen wiper that afternoon when the weather was much more reminiscent of summer. They'd left instruction with Ruth to monitor Hannah's every move, and for them to sleep in the same room. Hannah was to go nowhere without big sister. With every flash of lightning, the image of Nicola standing at the window accompanied, each time forcing Jack to shudder.

'I think it might be time to go back through that passenger list,' Jack said, waiting for the latest red light to change. 'If Nic and Hannah are struggling...'

'I can work through the list. Try to get contact details.'

'We only need a few and they're probably all local-ish, if they're using this airport. It's not big enough for people to travel miles for. That helps us. Start with the phone book. Then social media. That should give us enough.'

The light turned green and they set off again, The Star appearing up ahead as they rounded the next corner. Town was empty.

'I was thinking,' Cross started. 'Radiation poisoning fits

in with what you described with Nic. The hair loss, rash...' he tailed off to let Jack consider.

Jack shook his head. 'Thought about that myself. Hannah is fine. On the outside, at least. Self-harm is the more likely.'

Jack pulled up in the deserted carpark. The image of Nicola had shaken him, so far removed from his expectation was she. Jack was ready for a drink. Getting closer to the truth would just be a bonus.

'What are your hopes here?' Cross asked.

'Well, he didn't tuck his number under my wiper to tell me that he saw nothing. I suppose we're about to find out if your UFO theory holds any water.'

2

The pub was one of a chain where the inside of every one looked identical. Same menu, same carpet, same soundtrack playing in the background, beer bought in bulk by HQ to undercut every other pub in town. There was one near Jack's place. He never used it.

If Sean's idea was to meet here so that he'd be safer in a public place, it had backfired. Midweek, before the football season, pissing down outside. There were half a dozen people inside. Sean spotted two men walk in and case the place and raised a hand to show it was him. A lot younger than Jack expected, although he really had no idea how much training it took to become an air traffic controller. Jack took one look at Sean, sitting in the corner so he could see the whole room, leg bouncing under the table, and saw a man afraid.

He had something for them alright, and it was something big.

'He looks like he's shitting himself. Go and lay the charm on him, I'll get them in.'

Jack gestured across to Sean to see if he wanted a drink. Sean shook his head.

'Get me an IPA,' Cross said as he went across to speak to Sean.

'And don't start with the weird talk,' Jack said after him, before moving to the bar, eyeing the top shelf. After the day he'd had, he needed something stronger.

The barman (who looked pissed off new customers had come in so close to closing time) begrudgingly dispensed the drinks and Jack weaved to the table in the corner where Cross was calming the nervous Sean.

'Sean, I'm Jack Talbot. I've had a hell of a day, and I get the feeling you're not in the mood for chatting, so let's get down to business. That okay?'

Sean nodded, and swigged his coke. Jack sank half of his cheap Bourbon and Coke in one go.

'So, what have you got for us?'

Sean pulled out his mobile and clicked around the icons before setting it carefully on the table.

'I've got a video.'

Cross's eyes widened briefly until he regained composure and sipped his drink.

'Dave told me to contact you. Said you were helping one

of the passengers. I don't agree with what they're doing,' Sean said.

'What they're doing?' Jack asked.

'The hijacking story. It's all bullshit...'

He paused as the background music stopped between songs, waiting for the next latest pop wonder to cover their conversation.

'Anyway,' he continued, 'I was working the tower that night, and I've been at this a few years, but the guy I work with has been doing this forever and he says he's never seen anything like it. We were reviewing the radar return trying to find out what happened, and I managed to sneak a video.'

He scanned the room making sure nobody was watching, then picked up his phone and pressed play.

It was dark, with a green circle almost filling the frame. The arm swept around and a blip appeared.

'Okay so this is just before... That dot there,' he pointed with his pinkie, 'is one-eight-seven...'

Jack and Cross followed the flight.

Sean said, 'Keep watching. I knew the story on the news was bollocks when they said it was missing over the Channel. It never even got that far. We have to hand over to a different radar once they reach altitude. They never made it. They were still on our radar when it happened. Here it is...'

Jack watched the blips moving on the screen. 187 was on its own, nothing in its vicinity. No large second dot magically appearing. Nothing shooting in at incredible speed from nowhere. The arm swept again and 187 was still alone. Then,

THE VANISHING OF FLIGHT 187

it was gone.

'That's it?' Cross asked.

'That's it.'

Jack pressed further. 'Could it be they just turned the thing... the...'

'Transponder? No. If they turn that off, we still see the blip, just no data. That's how we knew it wasn't hijacked.'

Cross asked, 'So what did you think had happened?'

'Well, Ste...' Sean stopped and corrected himself, 'my mate... in the tower said that because there was nothing near it, it can't have been a collision. The only way you see what we've just seen is if the plane has exploded. The angle of the roof in the tower meant we couldn't see the flight with the naked eye, but we knew it was only a few minutes after take-off, so it was over land. A plane that size blows up over land, it's only a matter of minutes before the calls start coming in... when the news didn't come in, we were baffled.'

'Can you send me a copy of that video?' Jack said.

Sean nodded and they transferred a copy between their phones.

'Listen,' he said, again scanning the pub for threats, 'it took me a while to get in touch with you because Dave warned me... he said you followed him and stuff.'

'Don't worry Sean,' Jack replied, 'that was because he knew things he wasn't telling. I don't blame him. But we've got everything we need. If this is the last time you want to see us, then that's your choice. If there's anything else you can think of, or if you need any help, you know how to get in touch,'

'Thanks,' Sean said. 'I can relax a bit now. I wanted this off my mind. Jamie says I've been a right pain in the arse since this whole thing kicked off.'

'I think it's been rough on everyone it's touched. You only have to see us again if you want to. That's up to you.'

Sean's leg had stopped bouncing and he even managed a smile.

The barman called time at the bar and Jack and Cross rose.

'Take care Sean. Thanks again for the video, you've been a big help.'

'No offence, but I'll wait in here a minute. Don't want us to be seen leaving together.'

3

'Come on! You can't still believe that!' Jack scoffed at Cross. From what Jack had seen on Sean's video, the UFO theory was well and truly off the table.

The journey back to Jack's place had been silent while he worked through the new information provided by the video. He got the impression Cross didn't want to talk, but soon after they'd returned to Jack's place, they shared their ideas aloud.

'*We've* got planes that don't show on radar. If they're that technologically advanced, don't you think they'd be able to hide themselves from a radar?'

THE VANISHING OF FLIGHT 187

Jack shook his head. 'I've entertained that for long enough. If there had been something on that video, I might, *might*, have considered it. But now...'

'What then?' Cross challenged. 'If not a UFO. There was no explosion. No hijacking. Hannah Draper said she saw a flash. How do you account for that?'

Jack shrugged, 'I don't know. But there's still no physical proof that would say it has anything to do with flying saucers or little green men.'

'Little green men?! Who said anything about little green men?' Cross shouted.

Jack tried to diffuse the situation. 'Listen, I don't know about you, but I'm still a bit wired. How about we have a drink and start working through that passenger list? It's a bit late now, but we'll call Ruth first thing and show her the video.'

'I'll have a drink, but I still think you're wrong.'

'Well, it's a start,' Jack said, getting up and going into the kitchen.

He returned with two large bourbon and ice and they started their way through the passenger list, he at the top, Cross at the bottom, using phone book entries to get contact info for as many passengers as they could.

Jack took a swig from his glass. 'What a fucking day.'

Cross nodded. 'I'm still not talking to you.'

'Not talking to me?!' Jack replied. 'You're the one who used me to get into this craziness!'

'I've already apologised for that.'

'Well, I haven't accepted...' Jack said.

'Got one!' Cross replied. 'One out of six, but still...'

'Yeah,' Jack said. 'This job's not as easy as it used to be. Might have been a few years back we'd get info on half the passengers on that flight. Still, this might turn up half a dozen. We'll call them tom—'

His phone started ringing. Both men looked at the clock.

'It's one in the morning.' Cross said in disbelief.

Both knew there really was only one person it could be.

'Ruth. Is everything okay?' Jack said into his phone, under the watchful stare of Cross.

Jack frowned and gestured to Cross to get up.

'Which hospital? ...Don't worry ...We'll be there in twenty minutes.'

4

'I feel sick, Jack.'

Jack was trying to focus on the roads. The rain had finally stopped, but the roads were wet, and he was exhausted and close to the limit for drink driving.

'Do you want me to pull over?'

'No. Let's just get there.'

From the corner of his eye Jack saw Cross staring out of the window his head gently shaking back and forth.

'You did everything to make this as safe as possible, Danny.'

'A girl has just tried to kill herself, Jack.'

'Let's just see what they say at the hospital. It's probably just a cry for help.'

They burst into the waiting area for intensive care to find Ruth Draper sitting alone and clutching a balled-up tissue. The space was empty and eerily quiet. Most of the corridors were in darkness, giving the place a creepy abandoned vibe.

'Ruth,' Jack said softly, hoping not to startle the poor woman.

Ruth looked up. Jack saw a woman who didn't understand what was going on. Ever since she'd dropped her sister off at the airport, her world had turned upside down. Aside from the mystery of Hannah's flight dropping off the face of the earth for three days, her life had been threatened, and the lives of her children. Now her sister had attempted to take her own life.

'What's the latest?'

Ruth spoke vacantly, 'I only left her for a minute. That's all. A minute. There was so much blood...'

Jack and Cross sat beside her, neither knowing what to say for the best. It was Ruth Draper who spoke.

'I went to the bathroom. I'd been waiting... I was *sure* she was asleep. She must have been pretending...'

Ruth broke down in tears. Jack put a consoling arm around her shoulder, and she leaned into him.

'I came back and she was gone. She was on the floor in the kitchen, slumped in the corner. She'd gone for the knives. Slit her wrists. Lengthways. She'd tried using a key first, for crying out loud.'

Jack had seen his share of suicides. The amount of time it took someone to bleed out, if someone found them, chances were they'd be okay. Physically, at least. That was a single slit across the wrist. Going along the forearm usually meant it was more than a cry for help. This was bad.

'She's in the best place now,' Jack said. 'They'll know what to do.'

Ruth nodded on his shoulder. Blood transfusions, after the patch up. That's what would be going on now. Until she was stabilised.

'Can I get anyone a drink? I think we passed a machine.' Cross offered.

Ruth turned to him. 'You've done enough.'

Jack saw Cross's world fall apart in his eyes.

'I'll have a coffee, Danny. Can you give us a minute, Ruth?'

Jack followed Cross through the double doors and into the darkened corridor.

'She's wrong.'

'Is she?' Cross said. 'I've gone too far. The hypnosis. I shouldn't have pushed.'

'You forced nobody. You told her to forget everything when she woke up. You said yourself, this could be triggered at any time. It could have been the lightning from the storm...'

Cross turned away, but Jack had already seen the tears pooled in his eyes.

'Danny.'

THE VANISHING OF FLIGHT 187

Cross looked up.

'It's been a long day, and it doesn't look like it's going to get any shorter. Get us a couple of coffees. I'll have a word with Ruth. okay?'

His friend nodded and trudged away along the corridor. Jack shoved the door to the waiting area open.

'This is not his fault.'

Ruth looked around; eyebrows raised.

'We wanted answers. We all did. Him, me, Hannah... You.'

'Wait a minute—'

'No,' Jack said. 'You wait. There could be a hundred reasons this happened when it did. How it did. I saw Nic Lutton earlier. She's not in good shape. Daniel Cross is a good man. We're all in this now, together, whether we want it or not. We can get through it better. Together. The information Danny has got has proved that this is far from straightforward. But it's given me an idea of how we can get some sort of justice. That's not important now. What's important now, to all of us, is Hannah.'

Ruth nodded and a door swung open. A short bespectacled doctor appeared through one door as Cross emerged from another struggling with three cups of coffee.

Ruth stood and met the doctor as he neared. 'How is she?'

'She's stable,' the doctor said in an Eastern European accent. 'Not out of the woods yet, as you say. We'll keep her in overnight, just to be safe.'

'Can I see her?'

'I'm afraid not. There's not a lot you can do here. You should come back tomorrow.'

Ruth shook her head. 'I'm not leaving her again.'

The doctor nodded. 'I understand. There's a more comfortable waiting area. If you'd like to follow me.'

The three of them grabbed their coffees and set off behind the doctor. He stopped.

'It's for family members only, I'm afraid.'

Jack turned to Ruth. 'Will you be okay?'

Ruth nodded, 'Yes. Thank you for coming... both of you.' She turned to Cross. 'And thanks for the drink.'

Cross nodded.

'Call us if there's anything you need,' Jack said.

They stood and watched as the double doors swung closed behind Ruth.

'Do you think we should check on Nicola?' Cross asked.

Jack nodded. 'Sounds like a good idea.'

'What a night,' Cross sighed as they left the hospital, rubbing his tired face.

Jack glanced across, 'Do you want to go back to the flat? I can drop you off—'

'No, it's fine.'

Cross sipped at the coffee, checking the temperature before downing the contents of the paper cup. Jack nodded and smiled to himself. Cross loved this stuff. The work. Working with Tommy in the past had been great, but since he'd gone solo he'd got used to the idea of working alone. If there was one person he could work with in the future, that person would be Daniel Cross. Jack emptied the contents of his own cup, before glancing at the clock on the dash. Twenty past two in the morning. He knew how Cross felt: he needed sleep.

Any thought of going to bed anytime soon evaporated as he rounded the corner and turned into Nic Lutton's Street.

5

Jack pulled over behind the police car that sat in the street. The lights were off, and there was no ambulance. Jack hoped these were good signs. They burst from the car and stood at the end of the Lutton's driveway.

'What do you think?' Cross asked.

'No flashing lights, which means they've been here long enough to turn them off, or they weren't on in the first place, if I had to guess—'

Jack's sentence was cut short by the front door opening. Mr Lutton was shaking the hand of the tall WPC.

'Thank you.'

'If you think of anything, anything at all that might help, call us.'

The police strode down the driveway and Mr Lutton closed the door. Showing no interest in the two men standing at the end of his driveway at half past two in the morning.

'When did she go missing?' Jack asked the police.

The WPC replied, 'Sorry, who are you?'

'Friends of a friend. She was on the same flight. You do know about the flight?'

The police officers exchanged a look.

'We're not at liberty to discuss an ongoing case with members of the public,' the male policeman replied. 'What's your name?'

Jack stared at the constable. 'I'm not at liberty to discuss personal matters with officers of the law.'

The men stared at each other, like two gunslingers facing off.

'Let's go,' the WPC said, moving to the car.

Jack stared at the car until it was out of sight. The second it was gone, Jack turned to Cross.

'Nicola's gone.'

Cross replied, 'So let's look for her.'

Under the courtesy light, Jack spread a map of the area over his knees and held a pen over it, ready to draw.

'After everything the Luttons have been through this week, how long do you think they waited before calling the police?'

Cross replied, 'Search of the house, garden. No Nicola, call the police. Straight away, I'd say.'

'Right,' Jack confirmed. 'And how long do you think it took the police to arrive?'

Cross thought for a second, 'Quiet night. Midweek. Early morning. Half an hour, tops.'

'Agreed. That makes it one hour max since Nic went

missing, and the state I saw her in, I highly doubt she's driving. If she was, we'd never catch her anyway. But...'

He drew a circle on the map.

'She's within this circle. Somewhere. All we have to do, is find her.'

6

The clock showed just after four as they pulled away from the airport. Anyone turning up looking like Nicola would have drawn a lot of attention, so if she was there, finding her would have been easy. They crossed the airport off their very short list. Hannah's place and Ruth's had already drawn blanks and the streets in between were those of a ghost town.

'She could literally be anywhere,' Cross said, scanning the map.

'The police will have checked local hospitals. We could be here all night. How's about we go back to see how Hannah's doing before we call it a day?'

Cross reluctantly agreed and they headed back to the hospital, eyes scanning the route for the missing girl all the way.

Ruth looked like she'd managed a little sleep. She said they'd even let her in to see Hannah.

'How is she doing?' Cross asked.

'She seems fine. She doesn't remember any of it. That's how it is these days. Fine one minute, the next... They'll let her out in the morning... Later in the morning.'

'Do you still want to wait here?' Jack asked.

'I don't want to oversleep at home.'

'I think maybe you could use a little help. Do you have anyone?' Jack asked.

'Not really. Work have been great with me. Letting me take time off. But no. It's just me.'

Jack nodded. 'We'll call it a day for now. If I haven't heard from you in a few hours, I'll check in. Don't worry. We'll work something out.'

Ruth smiled. 'Thank you. Both. I don't know where I'd be.'

'Try to rest. We'll be in touch.'

Jack and Cross left Ruth and entered the car park, the morning sun reddening the horizon.

'I don't know how she's holding it together,' Cross said.

'Let's get some sleep. It's been a long day. And I've got a feeling tomorrow... today will be more of the same.'

'A feeling?' Cross asked.

'Shut up.'

'That sounds a bit... "spooky". '

'Shut up.'

Both men managed a smile as they fell into Jack's car and set off for HQ. All the way home they were on the lookout for Nicola. By the time they got back, the sun would be up. They'd have time for a few hours' sleep. Jack imagined that Hannah would be given sedatives to control her swings so that Ruth could finally get some rest.

A sound faded in, interrupting Jack's thoughts. In the

distance, faint at first, Jack heard something rising through the morning.

A wailing sound of not one, but two vehicles.

'What's this?' Cross said, his tone more like "What now?"

He knew as well as Jack did this was connected to whatever mess they were mixed up in. The sirens rose as a police car and ambulance screamed past them.

'Nicola?' Cross asked.

Without a word, Jack stepped on the accelerator and followed. Jack manoeuvred around cars in the wake of the emergency vehicles and followed in their slipstream.

'Ruth and the Luttons live in the opposite direction, hold on...' Jack sped up through a red light, then continued, and it's not near our security guy David...'

The breakneck pace kept up until they pulled into a housing estate. Nothing like Ruth's, more like David's, but somewhere in between. At the far end of the estate was a quiet cul-de-sac. They navigated behind the police car, neighbours dotting the street in pyjamas and dressing gowns.

They parked up and leapt out in pursuit of the police and paramedics.

'Where are you going?' the policeman challenged.

'We live here, number seventeen,' Jack said, not missing a beat. 'What's going on?'

The question was ignored, and the rush continued. Bleary-eyed residents leaned from doorways or peered from behind curtains, transfixed by the commotion that had shattered their early-morning quiet. Just as Jack and Cross reached the front door, it slammed shut.

'Shit!' Jack said, turning back to face Cross. 'Excuse me,' he shouted over Cross's shoulder.

Cross turned to the young woman next door. Jack strode along the street to the open doorway, the young woman pushing excited kids behind her at the door.

'I'm sorry to bother you, but that house, who lives there?'

She turned behind her for a moment, 'Will you shut up!' The excited chatter quietened, just for a moment, before starting up again at the same volume. 'I hope everything's okay. That's Sean's place.'

Jack saw Cross look at him. His stomach sank.

'Sean?'

'Sean Cook.'

'Sean who worked at the airport?'

'Yes,' she said. 'That's right.'

7

Jack stared through the windscreen into the streets before him. More neighbours had come out now, stunned chatter being exchanged up and down the road in a giant game of Chinese whispers. Jack and Cross went over everything they'd managed to get from the young mum before the screaming kids need for breakfast took over.

'New house, in a nice neighbourhood, wedding in a few weeks... this stinks to high heaven.'

'Let's just wait and see,' Cross said.

THE VANISHING OF FLIGHT 187

'When the police and an ambulance are rushing to a scene, it's never good.'

Jack's thoughts went back to the articles that Cross had been sending over the past few months. Stories of powerful people wanting something secret to stay that way, and unfortunate witnesses forcibly removed from the equation. But to admit that now meant that perhaps Cross's "out there" theories weren't so crazy after all. Cross removed the awkwardness for him.

'You don't think it was suicide.'

Jack shook his head. 'No. That's just it. I don't.'

The doorway darkened and the paramedics appeared with a stretcher. Whoever the poor soul on it was, they were draped in a white sheet.

'Oh Jesus. Is this real?'

Jack nodded. 'Life or death.'

'But I don't get it. Why? Why him and not Hannah or Nicola?'

'Shit.'

Jack went from deep thought to all action and fired the engine up.

'Where are we going?'

The car screamed away from the curb.

'We've got to make sure that what just happened to Sean doesn't happen to David.'

They raced across town in the early morning light to David's house.

Cross was gripping everything he could to stay in his

seat. 'What makes you so sure they'll go for him and not one of the girls?'

'Loose ends. Sean was one. David's one. People who know too much. The girls are non-compos mentis,' Jack yanked the wheel and they screeched around a corner. 'Nobody would believe them at this point because there's no physical evidence. But someone like Sean... All his marbles were in place, so if he opened his mouth...'

'What are we going to do? With David, I mean.'

Jack was scanning the streets, on the lookout for potential dangers as they rushed through the dawn. 'We'll get him out of town. Somewhere safe.'

'Doesn't all of this prove that something's afoot?' Cross asked.

'All circumstantial. Except for the video. Sean's death will look like an accident. Or a botched robbery.'

'So you'll admit that there's something weird going on?'

Jack sighed. 'It doesn't mean it was a UFO.'

Cross turned to Jack. 'What then?'

'Just because we can't explain it doesn't mean we should jump to conclusions about all manner of stuff.'

'I shouldn't need to remind you, Jack, what we saw...'

There it was. Out loud and inexplicable.

Jack had tried his best to bury the Laszlo Breyer experience into some forgotten corner of his mind. If it stayed there, he wouldn't have to acknowledge it. But Cross was right. He had seen it. So had his ex-partner Tommy, and Tommy's new partner Brian. The last he'd heard, Brian was still in therapy.

'It doesn't change anything, Jack.'

'Doesn't it?'

'Just because we saw what we saw doesn't mean we have to believe any old tosh we read about. It doesn't mean we didn't walk on the moon, and it certainly doesn't make the earth flat. We still need evidence. Proof.'

Cross was right. There was enough proof here to confirm that whatever they were dealing with was far from ordinary. But they didn't have enough proof, however much Daniel Cross wanted it to be true.

'It's all circumstantial.'

'You're right, Jack, I agree... I just think we should have open minds; once we've ruled out the conventional.'

Jack nodded. A tiny nod. An almost imperceptible nod. But it was a start.

They rounded the corner to David's street.

'Shit.'

8

They screeched to a halt outside David's place and leapt from the car.

'Careful, Cross,' Jack said marching along the path towards the front door of David's house.

The front door was wide open, the floor littered with splintered wood. Jack knew that the inside of the house would be ransacked, just as Sean's would have been. What he didn't know is if the people who'd done it were still here. And if they'd find David.

Jack entered first, wishing he had more than his fists to defend himself. He turned to Cross, 'Wait here, it might not be safe.'

'Bollocks to that. I'm coming in.'

Jack knew there was no point arguing. 'You take the upstairs then.'

Cross nodded and inched upstairs.

Jack shouted, 'David? Are you there, David?'

If there was anyone here, he didn't want Cross getting hurt in a case of mistaken identity. But there was no reply. Jack snuck into the living room. Whoever was here had done a real number on the place. Furniture smashed or overturned, drawers opened, contents scattered. He heard Cross shout David's name from upstairs as he crept into the dining room. Glass crunched underfoot, and the table and chairs were upended. Jack slowly peered over the top of the table, the image of David slumped in the corner, bullet hole in the middle of his forehead firmly imprinted into his mind's eye. He held his breath.

But the corner was just contents of the drawers. Smashed crockery and glasses. No David. The kitchen was empty too, which meant that if David was here, he was upstairs, and the chances of him being alive were almost zero.

'Jack?'

Jack raced to the foot of the stairs. Cross appeared.

'Nothing.'

Sirens rose in the distance.

'Let's get out of here, Danny. Maybe he's at work.'

Cross darted downstairs and the two of them raced back to the car.

'It was a real mess up there.'

'Whoever was looking for him here,' Jack said, 'Will go looking for him there. We just have to hope we get to him first.'

They jumped in the car and the tyres screamed as they fled. Jack glanced in his mirror as he neared the corner. A police car turned into the street. They'd missed them. Just.

9

They raced for the airport, morning sun now hovering above the horizon and throwing long shadows that stretched from the tree line towards the road. Jack hoped above hope that David was at work and not on some early morning errand, or he'd never find him.

'They'll get there before us, but they can't do anything while he's in there. While he's at work, he's safe.'

They were almost there, but it felt wrong for Jack not to rush.

'Shit.' Jack felt his face tingling.

'What is it?'

Jack reached into his pocket and said, 'Catch.'

Cross caught the mobile phone.

'Call Damien, make sure he's okay.'

Cross nodded and tapped at the phone. Jack snatched a ticket from the machine and the barrier rose.

'No answer.'

Jack pulled into the car park and headed for where David was parked the last time they'd been here. 'Keep trying.'

Cross was shaking his head. 'It's gone straight to voicemail.'

Jack gestured for the phone to be returned. 'Damien, it's Jack. As soon as you get this, call me.' Jack dialled the paper while scanning the parked cars before them. 'See it?'

Cross ducked and leaned trying to get an angle on David's car as someone at the paper picked up the phone.

'Can I speak to Damien Spade?' Jack peered over the cars in front looking for David's car himself. 'A friend... I'd rather not say... Yes, I'll wait...'

Cross pointed, 'There. Near the front.'

Jack extended himself like a meerkat so he could see where Cross was looking, and his eyes settled on the dark blue of an estate car.

'I'll go and pay for the ticket and check,' Jack said, climbing out.

He strode for the airport entrance, taking a detour in the direction of the blue car. The receptionist from the paper came back saying that Damien wasn't in the office and could she take a message. Jack hung up and pocketed his phone, scanning the area for other parties interested in this part of the car park, but there was no-one to be seen. The number plate of the dark blue car came into view and Jack scratched the side of his nose, hoping it would be enough for Cross to understand that the search for David's car was over.

Now they just had to wait for the man himself.

The terminal building was busy, finally back to business as usual, if only they knew what he did. Jack scoped for anyone out of place, though there was no one obvious. He slid coins into the ticket machine to cover the maximum stay; he wanted no hold ups when the time came to go. All the time he was hoping his phone would ring. That Damien would get in touch so that he could warn him. With Sean dead, it put all of them at risk, himself and Cross included, but there wasn't enough of him to go around to protect all of them. All he could hope was that his theory about the girls being the biggest danger to themselves was correct. As he entered the fresh morning of the car park, he toyed with the idea of sending Cross to Damien's place in a taxi, but questioned how safe Cross would be on his own.

Safety in numbers, Jack.

He got back into the car and focused his attention on the exit from where David had appeared before.

'Anything from Damien?' Cross asked.

'Not at the paper, not answering his mobile.'

'You don't think...'

Jack stared at the airport exit, sick to his stomach at the way this case was unfolding. 'Hard to say. Damien's streetwise, if nothing else...'

He didn't know what else to say. He was comforting Cross and himself more than anything. Damien was in just as much danger as David was, and as much as Sean had been. They were marked men, all of them, but Jack was wondering if Sean's demise was a result of leaking the video, or if word had somehow got out that he'd recorded it in the first place. Had Jack's work put others at risk?

'Do you think they'll approach David inside?' Cross said.

Jack had thought of this. The military man's MO was flying below the radar. While he was at work, David was safe. It was once he left—

All thoughts vanished from his head as a man with jet black hair emerged from the exit door at the side of the airport. David was alive, they just had to make sure he stayed that way.

CHAPTER SEVEN

DAVID STRODE ALONG the inside of the chain link fence, smiling at the security guard in the booth. His smile dropped when he saw Jack and Cross running towards him.

'For Christ's sake,' he said, voice lowered so the booth guard didn't hear. 'Are you trying to get me killed?'

'Quite the opposite,' Cross replied.

David frowned, before shoving past them. 'Leave me alone. I shan't tell you again. This is harassment.'

'Do you have a friend you can stay with, out of town for a few days?' Jack asked.

David marched on, pulling the phone from his pocket. 'I'm calling the police.'

Jack and Cross moved around him, blocking the path to his car. Any hopes Jack had of playing this low-key were as dead as poor Sean Cook.

'David, please.'

David stared at Jack; phone stuck to his ear. 'Hello, police please.'

'Sean is dead.'

David's mouth fell open and the phone slowly fell away from his ear, the tinny sound of the 999 operator still spilling from it.

Cross said, 'We've got to get you out of town, you could be in danger too.'

David slowly lifted the phone back to his ear. 'Sorry, it was the kids messing about.'

Jack spied over both shoulders before turning attention back to David. 'You need to get out of town for a few days while this all blows over.'

'And what if it doesn't "blow over"?' David barked.

'We don't have time to argue. Is there somewhere you can go?' Jack said.

'Christ.' David paced, hand rubbing at his forehead. 'What about them? The people I go to stay with. Am I endangering them?'

Jack reached into a pocket and produced a roll of twenties. 'A hotel then...' He counted out the notes stopping at three hundred. 'Somewhere cheap. Out of the way. Somewhere you'll be safe.'

David paused. He looked at Jack and then Cross, before snatching the cash.

'Good,' Jack said. 'Let's go. We'll escort you out of town, make sure you get out okay.'

David just nodded.

'Come on. Let's move,' Jack said, urging everyone into action.

They sprinted to their separate cars, Jack waiting for David to set off before following.

'What happens next? After we've got David out? We can't protect him forever.'

'I'm working on that,' Jack replied, stuffing his parking ticket into the barrier. 'One step at a time, eh?'

David was wasting no time in getting away, snaking from the monochrome of the airport, around the roundabout and towards the traffic lights leading to green countryside ahead. Just as David approached, the lights switched from a welcoming green to red. Jack pulled up behind as David revved his engine and glanced in the mirror. Jack gestured for him to calm down. His mind went back to the articles Cross had sent. UFOs. Conspiracy. Before, he'd written them off as rubbish, but now he doubted exactly how safe David would be if he ended up in police custody. The last they needed was to get pulled over for traffic violations. The light changed and Jack glanced in his mirror in time to see a familiar black car.

David turned left and Jack followed, all the while eyeing the mirror hoping he'd been mistaken.

'Shit.'

Cross turned, 'What?'

Jack looked in the mirror as the black car pulled onto the road behind them. The same car he'd met at the industrial estate.

'We've got company.'

2

Jack peered in his mirror again before flashing his headlights at David. They were in big trouble and David had no idea how much. David glanced back and Jack pointed forwards, closing the space between his car and David's. The security guard needed no second invitations. He floored the accelerator and sped away.

'Seatbelt,' Jack said as Cross nodded and reached across himself.

Jack was close behind David, and David was wasting no time, weaving around cars whenever the opportunity presented. Another glance in the mirror revealed their new friends were still behind them.

'They aren't playing games.'

'It's broad daylight,' Cross replied, incredulous at the audacity of their pursuers.

Jack yanked the wheel to round the latest obstacle in the road, this one sounding his horn at them.

'I know these bastards,' Jack said.

'From where?'

'The industrial estate a few nights back.'

The small winding road carried on ahead before opening into two lanes of dual carriageway peppered with light early morning traffic.

'I don't like this,' Jack said.

'Being chased in broad daylight?'

Jack raced along behind David, who wasn't quite as fast as Jack thought. He seemed more confident closer to the airport, but here on the open road, Jack had gained on him. The car behind had gained on Jack.

'If I were these guys, I'd have a roadblock set up on here. It's easy enough to arrange. The smaller roads... there's too many of them, and not enough police. We need to get off here, fast.'

Jack pulled in as close as possible behind David and as soon as the road ahead was clear, flashed his lights. Jack pointed to the next exit. David shook his head. Jack glanced in the mirror and saw the black car weaving behind the cars they'd already passed. The gap was closing.

'Fuck's sake.'

Jack hit the horn and pointed again. David slammed both hands against the steering wheel.

'I need to block their view,' Jack said, keeping as close to David as he could. 'If they don't see him leave the road, they'll follow us.'

The exit came and David left the main road. Jack had done his best to block the view. He glanced in the mirror, desperately hoping for some clue. If he turned now and they hadn't caught sight of David, he'd be leading them straight to him.

'Go straight,' Cross shouted.

But Jack wasn't sure. If they had seen David, he'd be on his own.

'Shit!' Jack yelled, before yanking the wheel, turning onto the same exit David had taken.

The black car followed.

The smaller country road was empty. They were exposed. It would be easy for them to disappear here. Anything bad happening here could easily be made to look like an accident.

'At least they can't get past us,' Jack said aloud, sure that Cross was following his train of thought.

A *bang!* came from behind. Jack and Cross both looked at the mirrors. Jack knew from the sound there could only be two possibilities. The first was a blowout. It wasn't his. An exploded tyre on the car behind would end the chase. That would be lucky. The other option…

'Gun!' Cross shouted.

A pistol was aiming from the passenger window. Another *bang!* sounded and the rear windscreen exploded.

'Jesus! Get your head down!'

Cross ducked and Jack focused on David's car. If they slowed, they could stall their pursuers just enough for David to escape. But it was going to get rough.

'Hold on to something.'

The black car was close now. Close enough for Jack to see the faces of the men driving. He expected to see the military man from Cross's sketch, but he was neither driver nor gunman. Their military friend got his minions to do his dirty work. He liked to stay in the shadows. He's powerful in the shadows.

The black car's engine screamed as it sped alongside Jack.

'Hold on!' he screamed, moving to block them.

Bang!

Another gunshot. Jack felt the bullet whistle past his ear. The front windscreen exploded into a spiderweb.

'Jesus!' Cross shouted.

The black car was directly behind them. Jack slowed to block them off, David's car was smaller now, visible through the mosaic of windscreen, escaping to freedom down the road.

Thud!

There was a jolt and the steering wheel tried to free itself from Jack's grasp.

'Fucking shunting us,' Jack shouted over the noise; engines and wind and gunfire, all vying for attention. A corner approached.

A shunt like that on the corner…

Jack wasn't sure he could hold on. He sped into the corner, pulling away from their pursuers. Another gunshot rang out and Jack ducked as he turned the wheel. Tyres screeched and the smell of burning rubber filled the car.

By the time they'd got around the corner, David was almost at the next one. He was close to escape. As soon as they were on a straight road, Jack slammed the breaks.

'Hold on!'

A dull thud and a smash of headlights filled the air as the black car smashed into them. If Jack could keep this up for a few more minutes…

David vanished around the corner, but if the black car reached that same corner, they'd still be able to see him. From where David had vanished a white van appeared, heading towards them. Jack prayed they wouldn't be drawn into the firing line.

'You okay, Danny?'

Jack glanced at Cross.

'Danny!'

Cross's head lolled lazily to one side. The front of his shirt was wet, blooming red.

THUD!

Another hit from behind. The rear wheels came out from under them and Jack yanked the wheel against the turn. He'd straightened up, but the engine of the black car was screaming again, dragging it alongside Jack.

He glanced as the car pulled alongside, the passenger taking aim. He jerked the wheel and slammed into the side of the black car just as the gun went off. The bullet ripped through the frame of the windscreen. Jack glanced across. They'd lost control. They swerved from side to side as the van gained on them. He hit his horn and at the last moment, they swerved. Jack waited for the crash, but none came. When the van had passed, they were at the other side, waiting.

The van sped away, leaving Jack and MI-whoever to get on with it. Jack floored the gas and aimed right for them. He slammed into them and this time, there was no coming back.

The tyres screeched and the car flew into a ditch. The wheels caught the ridge at the far side, sending the car rolling on impact.

Jack slammed the breaks and watched as the black car tumbled and rolled, over and over - roof, chassis, roof, chassis - finally settling upside down forty yards away in the field.

He turned attention to his friend.

'Cross!'

The blood was pouring from his shoulder. He was out cold, the right side of his chest a deep red and spreading down his abdomen. Jack glanced in the mirror to make sure whoever it was trying to kill them was not readying themselves for another attempt. But instead of seeing people coming from the overturned car, he saw flames.

Jack opened the glove compartment and grabbed the rag he kept in there for wiping the windscreen. The road was silent. No van behind. No David in front. Jack pressed the rag against Cross's gunshot wound and the crackle of flames drifted in from the field. The burning car was now engulfed in flames. Screams came from inside. He unfastened his seatbelt, then looked again at Cross. He couldn't leave him. The crackle of fire grew louder, and the screaming faded as Jack reached for his mobile.

He glanced at the burning car as the phone rang in his ear.

'Is that the hospital? I'm bringing a patient in, he's lost a lot of blood... Er, car accident. No, I can't wait for an ambulance... Because he'll fucking die! I'll be there in ten minutes.'

He ended the call and sped away. In his rear-view mirror, he saw what was left of the black car explode into a fireball.

3

'Danny? Stay with me, Danny.'

Jack shouted as he weaved through morning traffic, with one hand pressed against the rag on Cross's blood-soaked shirt. Horns blasted as Jack ignored lights and signals and warnings. Nausea rose in his throat. Daniel Cross might die right here, because of a case he was working on. It was all too familiar. Cross was not responding, his head lolling from side to side as Jack traversed the morning rush en route to the hospital.

He squinted through the smashed windscreen as the approaching light switched from amber to red, but rather than slow down, Jack floored it. This would not, could not, wait.

'Danny!' he shouted again.

There was still no response. Jack was trying to keep it from his mind that after he got Cross to the hospital, he wouldn't be able to stay. Once they found out it was a gunshot, and they'd have to call the police. If the police questioned him, his hands would be tied. He'd be in custody. He'd be in danger. Ruth, Hannah, Damien, Nicola, they'd all be on their own. This thing had to end, sooner rather than later. He couldn't end it from a cell. As soon as word reached the police that Military Intelligence was involved it would all be swept under the rug, and God alone knew what would happen to Jack then. Abandoning Cross now would leave Jack open to being framed for Danny's

death

injuries, but it was a risk he'd have to take. Cross would be getting the best care available, that was all that mattered.

Jack ignored the "Ambulances Only" sign and sped to the double doors. He jumped out of the car and two paramedics shouted at him.

'Help me!' Jack shouted as he rounded the car to Cross's door.

The paramedics rushed to help, grabbing the gurney from their parked ambulance.

'He's been shot in the shoulder,' Jack said. 'He's lost a lot of blood.'

Jack watched, head in hands, as they lifted his limp body onto the gurney.

'Sir?'

Are you listening to us, Jack?

'His blood type? What—'

'I don't know! I don't know his blood type.'

'Do you know his name?'

Jack hoped they'd be able to get his files from the system. 'His name is Daniel Cross. He's from York. That's all I know.'

The paramedics charged through the double doors, and Jack yelled after them.

'I'll just grab his bag from the car.'

Of course, there was no bag. He watched as they sprinted along the corridor before turning out of sight. Sean was dead, and Damien was missing. David was safe but who knew for how long. Jack watched Daniel Cross, blood-soaked and barely clinging to life as he vanished into the depths of the hospital. Jack wondered if he'd ever see his friend alive again.

4

Jack paced his living room and heard the approaching footsteps echoing along the hospital corridor on the other end of the phone.

'Yes?'

'I brought my friend in earlier. The gunshot victim.'

'Yes, the nurse told me. Your friend...' he started.

Jack was powerless. How many times he'd been on the other end of this speech, doling out the good or bad news to awaiting loved ones.

'...Your friend's condition is serious. But stable.'

A wave of relief came followed by the onrush of emotions. Jack drew a deep, haltering breath. He hadn't cried since Jenny's funeral.

'He's an incredibly lucky man. We're dealing in minutes. If his reaching this hospital had been delayed, I could be giving you very different news. I tell you this to highlight the long road to recovery your friend is facing, and it's a road with many pitfalls. He's lost a lot of blood. He's in an induced coma. The next twenty-four hours are vital.'

'Is there anything I can do?'

'If you are a religious man, you might pray.'

Christ, this was more serious than he'd anticipated. His head was light, and his eyelids heavy. He hadn't slept since yesterday morning. Jack should have been there, at the hospital, but he couldn't. They had no doubt called the police, and they were probably listening in on the conversation. Maybe even there by the phone with the doctor. If he tried to persuade Jack to turn himself in, he could be sure of it.

'Your friend is in the best place. Sir...' he began.

'I had no part in this. We were chased. The police will

find out what happened here and absolutely nothing will come of it, doctor, mark my words. This is bigger than you can imagine. All of you. I'm worried about my friend's safety.'

There was a pause. 'Sir, if you could just come in—'

Jack hung up. He was exhausted. But he couldn't sleep. Not now. This is where it had come to. Life or death. A point Hannah had already reached, attempting to take her own life just a few hours before, and Jack's racing mind wondered how many of the other passengers had already succeeded where Hannah had failed.

Since he'd returned home, he'd heard nothing from Damien, and had to expect the worst. Nic Lutton was missing. At least they'd been able to get David to safety. Jack didn't mind waiting, or how long it took, now that he knew that Cross had survived, his mind turned to one thing.

Revenge.

No sooner had the thought appeared, his phone rang.

5

Jack pulled his mobile from his pocket, expecting to find the latest instalment in a long line of bad news. It was a number he didn't recognise.

'Jack?'

Relief took the strength from Jack's legs.

'Damien. Thank Christ. I've been trying to reach you.'

'I've been busy,' he said.

Jack detected distraction in his voice, but before he could

question it, Damien spoke.

'Why? What's going on?'

Jack twitched the blinds and looked out into the street below. No unusual cars. He wondered how long it would be before they tracked him down. 'It's Cross. He's in hospital.'

'Hospital?'

Whatever it was Jack had sensed in Damien's voice before was gone. Empty shock was all that remained.

'He's been shot.'

'Jesus.'

'Listen, you need to watch yourself. We're in trouble.'

There was a short pause. 'What do you mean, Jack?'

'My source from the tower is dead, and they came after the security guard, tried to do the same. I was calling to make sure you were okay.'

'Shit, sorry. I've been snowed under working that bullshit story Rob gave me, had to turn my phone off. Then just as I walked in ten minutes ago, a call came into the newsroom, and I had to call you.'

'What is it?'

'One of my sources on the force. I'm on my way to the scene now. It's the Lutton girl.'

'Nicola?'

'She's dead.'

First Sean. Now Nicola. Hannah had already tried and failed. And Cross was fighting for his life. It was a matter of time before they came for Damien. And him. But Jack was tired of being on the back foot. He needed to turn things around. And to do that, he'd need Damien's help.

'Tell me where, I'll meet you.'

6

Jack downed his coffee and snatched up his car keys. The bridge Damien had told him about was twenty minutes away.

The last time he'd set eyes on the Lutton girl, he felt for her. She'd gone from being bright and beautiful and full of life to an empty shell. Clumps of hair missing; drawn, pallid features; arms bandaged from wounds that Jack had to presume were self-inflicted. It was as if something in her mind had snapped.

They were systematically removing witnesses. Sean. David. Nic. It was a matter of time before they got to Hannah.

Jack arrived at the scene. An old railway bridge in a quiet part of town, trees and fields all around. The police were interviewing the Luttons, and a body covered in a sheet was already being loaded into an ambulance by the railway below. They were working fast. The body could provide clues as to what happened, yet here it was just one more piece of evidence to be swept under the rug.

Damien saw him and waved. Jack waved back and parked near the young reporter.

'Suicide,' Damien said as Jack approached.

'Are you sure?' Jack replied, not believing it for a second.

'Apparently.'

'Do you think they've been got to?' Jack rubbed a hand

against the growth of stubble on his chin, and in a corner of his mind, a flag went up.

That's important.

Damien shrugged as he looked over to the couple sitting on the curb wrapped in a foil blanket. 'Hard to say,' he said, looking back at Jack. 'I'm just waiting for that copper to go so I can speak to them. What the fuck happened with Cross?'

'Yeah, that's what I wanted to talk to you about.' Jack moved ever so slightly closer to Damien and lowered his voice. 'You need to watch yourself.'

Damien nodded, but seemed unmoved.

'I'm working on something. Something that will put us onto the front foot, will you help?'

'Of course,' he said, not skipping a beat.

'Now's your chance,' Jack said nodding at the Luttons as the officer interviewing them moved away.

Jack watched on as Damien approached the couple, and his heart hurt for them. They'd lost their daughter twice in the same week and been fed bullshit as to what was really going on. Whatever Jack's plan was, he had to make sure they were looked after. With Nic murdered, it was doubtful they'd see any of the hush money.

The hush money...

Damien was met with shaking heads and was trudging back towards Jack when he set off in the opposite direction.

'Let me have a go,' Jack said as he passed Damien.

He approached the Luttons, but as he got close, Mr Lutton looked up.

THE VANISHING OF FLIGHT 187

'No interviews.' His tone was final.

Jack held up his hands, 'I'm not with the press. I'm a friend of Hannah Draper.'

At once, a wall seemed to come down. They knew whatever they'd been going through was happening to their little girl's best friend.

Jack stepped closer and a voice came from behind.

'Excuse me.'

Jack turned to see the officer who'd taken their statement.

'You can't—'

'It's fine,' Mrs Lutton said.

The officer stared at Jack. Jack stared back. He'd been through too much this morning to be intimidated by a stare and a badge. The officer backed down and turned away.

Jack watched him walk a few steps before turning back. 'I think I can help Hannah. But I just need a little information... if that's okay...'

Mrs Lutton nodded. Her husband couldn't even bring himself to look up.

Jack focused on Mrs Lutton. The past few days had taken a toll on her. The lines on her face showed as much.

'My name is Jack Talbot. I want to get the people responsible for killing Nic.'

'She wasn't killed.' Mr Lutton looked up. 'It was suicide.'

Jack was taken aback. 'I'm sorry to ask, but are you sure?'

'Nic loved to come here,' Mrs Lutton said. 'When she was little, we'd bring her here, walk through the woods. We'd have a picnic and play...'

Mr Lutton continued. 'We'd stay most of the day and then when the light was fading, we'd come up here. We'd watch the sunset before going home.'

Jack stood motionless and listened.

'We hadn't done it for years. But every now and then we'd talk about it. Talk about it and say we'd come back, but we never did...' Mr Lutton started to cry.

'I'm so sorry,' Jack said.

Mrs Lutton continued. 'We remembered how much she loved it here. We came as soon as the idea... but we were too late. When we got here, she was standing on the bridge, facing the road. She was smiling, like she was back there, as a little girl. I shouted her but, she leaned back. She was still smiling...'

Mrs Lutton broke down in tears. There was no doubt. It was suicide. But the military man had to be linked somehow, Jack could feel it. He reached into his pocket and pulled out the sketch.

'Just one more thing. Have either of you seen this man?'

Both looked up but shook their heads. Every time Jack tried to shine light onto this case, the further it retreated into the shadows.

'Thank you very much for your time. I'm sorry for your loss.'

'How is she?' Mrs Lutton asked. 'Hannah.'

Jack smiled a little. 'She's okay. She's been through a lot. I want to help her find the people responsible.'

Mr Lutton spoke, 'And you think it's him?' he pointed at the sketch.

'One of them, yes...' Jack paused, but knew he'd never get a better chance to ask. 'Would you mind if I took your number? It would be a big help.'

Both Luttons nodded and Jack scribbled down their number.

'Thanks again. Take care.'

Jack turned and headed back towards Damien, throwing a glance at the officer who'd tried to stare him down moments before. He wanted these bastards badly.

He walked past Damien and without looking at him said, 'Follow me.'

Jack Talbot was tired of being hunted. The time had come to turn the tables.

7

'What did you say to them? To get them talking I mean.' Damien asked the moment Jack closed the door to his flat.

Jack paused and chuckled.

'What?'

'"Vic Whisperer" Tommy used to call me,' Jack said dropping his keys to his desk. 'Said I could get any victim to talk to me. Just got one of those faces I suppose.'

Damien slumped to the settee.

'Who's Tommy?'

'My old partner when I was on the force. Haven't seen him for a bit...'

Jack's mind went back to the last time they spoke - after the fallout of the Laszlo Breyer case. How they'd patched things up as best they could but had barely spoken since.

'Listen,' Jack said, shaking the memory from his mind, 'I don't know about you, but I need caffeine.'

Damien nodded. 'Milk and two please.'

Jack wandered into the kitchen.

'So do you believe them?' Damien shouted from the living room. 'The Luttons, I mean. About the suicide.'

Jack waited until the kettle was watered before answering.

'Yes. Yes, I do.'

The look in the eye of Mr Lutton said he'd have been the first to cry foul if Nic's death had gone down any way other than they'd described. He wanted what Jack wanted. Justice.

'So what happens—'

Jack cut him off, shouting over the rising noise of the boiling kettle, 'Come in here if you want to talk to me.'

A few moments later Damien entered.

'I was just going to ask what happens now.'

Jack stared down at the mugs, waiting for the water to boil. 'Hannah and Nic have both attempted suicide. They did it at different times though. And Nic looked like the whole flight had taken a much worse toll on her than Hannah.'

'So...'

'So, chances are that if Nic and Hannah have attempted

suicide, others will too. Some of them might have already been successful. We need to work through that passenger list of yours and warn as many people as possible. We could use their help as well...'

The kettle finally clicked, and Jack stirred the water into the mugs, drawing deep breaths of rich coffee aroma as he did. He turned and planted a mug in front of Damien who'd now seated himself at the kitchen table.

'What was that picture you showed them? A police sketch?'

'Sort of.' Jack sipped at the scolding coffee. He sat across from Damien. 'Cross did it. He hypnotised the Draper girl.' Jack reached into his pocket and pulled out the folded sketch, tossing it across the table to Damien.

Jack watched as Damien unfolded the paper. His eyes widened. 'I know him.'

'From where?' Jack knew it was the press conference that he and Cross had been refused entry to at the airport, but he didn't want to influence the answer.

'I've seen him. Shit. Where was it?'

'At home, at work, at the airport, at—'

'The airport. That's it. Remember when the flight came back? They had that press conference. They wouldn't let you in.'

'The press conference.'

'You asked me if I'd seen him, but I couldn't remember.'

'And you're sure that's him?'

Damien was nodding slowly, deliberately. 'One thousand

per cent.'

'Good. That's good.'

Jack started to think about how this could be used. He had to take the fight to them somehow...

'Jack?'

Jack looked up from his coffee. 'Yes. Sorry. What?'

'The list?'

Jack stood from the table and lifted his coffee. 'Yes. Let's crack on. Actually, before that, I've got a job for you.'

Jack paced the living room while Damien sat on the settee, phone pressed against his ear.

'Yes. Daniel Cross... He was brought in this morning... My name?'

Damien looked up at Jack, who gestured in no uncertain terms that Damien should not divulge his identity. Damien got the hint.

'Pete Mitchell... Yes, I'll hold.'

Damien covered the microphone and looked up at Jack. 'They've gone to check.'

'They've gone to get the police. Or someone.'

Damien removed his hand from the microphone and spoke, 'This is he. Who am I?' Damien mouthed "for fuck's sake" at Jack before raising his voice. 'Is my friend okay, yes or no? It's a simple enough question.'

Damien smiled and covered the mic. 'He's fine.' He gestured that whoever was on the other end of the phone was yapping constantly, 'Yes thank you. That'll be all.'

THE VANISHING OF FLIGHT 187

Damien ended the call cutting off whoever was on the other end mid-sentence before putting his phone back in his pocket.

'What did they say?'

'They were more interested in who I was than telling me about Cross. But he's stable.'

'Good. I need you to do that every couple of hours. Let me know if there's any change.'

'No problem.'

They started to work through the list, finishing the work that he and Cross had started the night before. Jack told Damien about the run in with the black car, first at the industrial estate, and then the morning's events. Jack was concerned that another attempt might be made on Cross, once it was discovered who he was and what he'd seen. After a couple of hours, the first part of the list was done.

'Now what?' Damien asked.

'We call. Pretend to be a mobile phone provider. Ask if they've had any problems with the network. If they answer and sound fine, put a tick. If a depressed family member answers, put a cross. If we get no answer, put nothing. Once that's done, you start looking up on the crosses, obituaries, local news websites, anything. See what you can find out.'

'You mean see if any of the other passengers are dead?'

'Right.'

A sweep through the list yielded enough data. Just under half of the list didn't answer at all, but between the rest, there were more ticks than crosses. After the first few crosses turned up, Jack finished the calls, Damien moved onto digging. By the time they'd finished, it was two in the afternoon.

'Well,' Damien said, 'that was a waste of time.'

It wasn't a complete waste of time. The contact info, Jack would put to use on the next phase of his plan.

'Nothing?'

'Dead people? Not a sausage. Nothing in the obits. Found a couple in the hospital, failed attempts I imagine. That was hard work. Whatever it is that's going on, they don't want it out.'

'That, my boy,' Jack smiled, 'is how we beat them.'

8

'You know what you're doing?' Jack was staring at Damien.

Both men had before them two lists: a list of the passengers who were still alive, and a list of instructions.

'Yes. Get back in touch with as many ticks as possible. Tell them to await the call.'

Jack stared, 'And you remember your "in"?'

'Money, baby. It's always money.'

'Don't fuck about.'

'Relax, Jack,' Damien whined.

Jack scowled. 'Damien. Look at me.'

Damien looked up, straight faced, but his eyes were smiling.

'This is important. For all of us.'

The cheeriness finally fell away from his face. 'Don't worry. I'm on it.'

Jack was too tired for this.

'We only need half a dozen. But if we can get twenty, we take twenty. Got it?'

'Got it.' Damien looked at his list, then at Jack. 'What is it? What's so important that they'd kill to keep it quiet?'

'It's not a hijacking.' Jack replied.

'Well that's for fucking sure. I didn't ask you what *wasn't* going on.'

'I've got one theory...'

Damien shrugged.

Jack thought how pleased Cross would be to hear what Jack was about to say. He sighed. 'It sounds mental.'

'Jack. We've just got back from a bridge where a woman jumped to her death, not because she was sad or depressed. Because her plane went missing for three days. And then came back. Cross was shot. In broad daylight. Whatever it is, can't be worse than that.'

Jack's thoughts went back to the shit-smeared message on Nic Lutton's wall. That and the articles that Cross used to send him. Most of them sounded crazy at the time. If he read them again now...

'Jack?'

'Have you heard of Simulation Theory?'

Damien shook his head.

'What about the allegory of the cave?'

'Allegory of the what?'

Jack swigged his latest cup of coffee and started. 'Bear with me on this. I'm trying to recall it from something Cross sent me a few months ago, but basically, imagine two men chained with their eyes fixed forwards. They're in a cave. They can't see each other, can't look up, down, left, right. They can hear each other, but the only thing they've ever known is the cave wall in front of them.'

'Following so far.'

'Now imagine that somewhere in the cave behind them, is a fire. Small. A campfire. Between that fire and the wall they can see, people are walking back and forth, going about their business. To our prisoners, those shadows on the wall are all that is.'

'So they can only see two dimensions?'

'Bingo. Up, down, left, right. No depth. Just those two dimensions.'

'Okay...' Damien said, urging Jack to keep going.

'Now imagine one of our prisoners escapes. He breaks free of his chains and all of a sudden, he can turn his head. He sees the man next to him, the fire behind him. The people walking around. He makes a run for it and reaches the mouth of the cave. He sees fields and mountains and a sky full of stars. Then, he gets captured. He's taken back to his chains and his wall and his friend. So, the question is this: how does he describe the three-dimensional world to his friend? His 2D mind can barely process what it's seen, let alone find the words to describe it.'

Damien sat chewing on the idea for a second. 'Shiiiiiit.

THE VANISHING OF FLIGHT 187

You couldn't do it. You'd go mental... fucking hell.'

Jack drank his coffee. Now he didn't feel so tired. He'd got a second wind from somewhere.

Damien stood up. 'Wait a minute? Are you trying to tell me that Flight 187 went to another fucking dimension?'

'I've looked at all of the information in front of me, and it's the only thing that makes sense.'

'Makes sense?! It's fucking bananas!' Damien started pacing the floor.

Jack stood. 'When we hypnotised Hannah, she described seeing a flash inside the plane. We asked her to describe what she saw, and she flipped out. All she could say was, "I can't. I can't." Over and over. At first I thought it meant she couldn't see. Now I think the words she needed to describe what she was seeing just weren't there.'

'I can't,' Damien said, distantly.

'Those were the same words Nicola Lutton had scrawled on her wall. And think about this: how many of the passengers were men?'

'More than half.'

'More than half. How long was the flight missing?'

'A few days.'

'Be specific Damien. How long?'

'Three days.'

'Right. A flight goes missing for three days - a flight we know wasn't hijacked, because it completely vanished off radar, we're agreed on that?'

'Yes.'

'When those passengers returned, how many of the men were clean-shaven?'

Damien stopped dead.

'You've supposedly been kidnapped by hijackers and kept from your family for three days, not knowing if you're going to live or die; are you really going to stop and ask for a shave before you're reunited?' Jack looked at Damien. 'Would *you* stop and ask for a shave?'

'No,' he said quietly. 'No I wouldn't.'

'Planes get hijacked. Blown up. People are bastards. These are easy concepts to understand. If people start to think that their flight might just vanish into another dimension, they might not take the news too well. Why did it happen now? Where is this other dimension? Has it happened before? *Will it happen again?* People start asking questions like that, what happens when the best and brightest minds on the planet have to throw their hands up and say, "We don't know"?'

'Panic.'

'Not panic. *Chaos*. Chaos. All of a sudden going to work and paying your taxes don't seem that important. Society as we know it could collapse. *That's* what they're willing to kill for to keep secret.'

The room was overtaken by a stunned silence. For a moment, even the cars outside stopped going by.

Jack's phone rang.

Damien jumped. 'Fucking shit myself.'

Jack grabbed his phone. 'Hello?' He felt his smile melt

away, 'It's okay. It's going to be fine... I'll be there in ten minutes. Stay calm... Call the police.'

Jack put his phone back into his pocket.

'What's going on?' Damien asked.

'Are you going to be okay with this?' Jack said, gesturing at the lists of phone calls.

'Yes, what's wrong?'

Jack was already at the door, car keys in hand. 'It's Hannah Draper.'

9

Once again, Jack Talbot found himself rushing to Holly Drive. It was less than a minute since he'd set off when his phone went off again.

'Fuck's sake.'

He pulled the phone out and put the call on speakerphone.

'Jack?'

'Damien. What is it?'

'I was thinking, wouldn't it be better if I helped you look for Hannah?'

The traffic was light, and Jack had a clear run of the road. Something to be thankful for. His biggest concern right now should be the safety of Hannah Draper, but it was Damien carrying out the plan as he'd asked. He hadn't had time to explain exactly what each step was for, but if Damien missed one of them, getting people on board would be difficult. They needed all the help they could get.

'Finding Hannah saves one person. The plan, if it works, saves everyone. But the clock is ticking, Damien. This is really important.'

It dawned on Jack that he hadn't told Ruth about Nic. Maybe that was a good thing. Knowing that her sister's friend had thrown herself off a bridge a few hours ago would have done nothing to calm her nerves. As for Hannah...

'You think she's already dead, don't you?'

'That's not it,' he lied. 'We don't have the time or the manpower. I'll do everything I can for Hannah, but she needs you to get that list together. We all do. Okay?'

Silence.

'Damien.'

'Yes okay I'll do it.'

Damien put the phone down. Jack could only hope he did as he was asked.

Jack pulled into Holly Drive to find Ruth out on the front lawn. He drew up alongside her and jumped out of the car. Ruth was ragged. Tired. A woman at the end of her rope.

'She seemed fine. She said she had to go to the bathroom. I waited and knocked, and the window was open and—'

'It's not your fault. Have you called the police?'

Ruth nodded and wiped her nose on the ball of tissue kept in her sleeved hand.

'How long is it since she went?'

Ruth shook her head. 'Five, maybe ten minutes.'

'And she's on foot?'

'Yes.'

Ruth was frantic. It was clear she had the same feelings Jack did. Thank Christ she didn't know about Nic.

'If she's on foot she can't be far.'

Ruth whipped her head up at Jack. 'She could be anywhere, Jack.'

Her eyes had that same empty look he'd seen in the eyes of Nic's parents'. The image of them huddled together on the curb by the railway bridge…

Jack looked at Ruth. 'I think I might know where she is.'

CHAPTER EIGHT

RUTH WAS SITTING beside Jack, but the empty roads a few moments ago were gone and now peppered with cars going nowhere fast.

'It's the next left,' Ruth said.

The light turned red. They stopped.

'Are you sure this is the place? Can you think of any other—'

'No.' The old Ruth was back. Certain. Sure. 'This is the place. This is it.'

They were heading just outside of town. For the station. The lights changed and Jack screeched away.

'We'd always take train rides with mum and dad as kids. The four of us. We never knew where we were going. It was a big adventure. The trips stopped after mum died. Hannah always said how much she missed it, the days when all of us were together. This has to be it.'

The station came into view in the distance, car park full and filling further still with cars filtering off the main road. They hadn't passed her yet, but with the head start she'd got, she could be here already. The lights changed from green to amber with only one car between them.

'Come on, foot down.'

The car in front slowed. Jack slammed the horn, but the light turned from amber to red and the car stopped completely.

'Shit!' Ruth shouted.

'Come on,' Jack said, unbuckling his seat belt.

Ruth did the same and then they were both sprinting for the station, red light and beeping horns behind them.

'Was there a usual platform you went from?' Jack asked as they burst into the shade of the cold station building.

'Four,' Ruth replied, already leading them in the right direction.

They raced down the stairs and into the passage leading to the platforms, dodging wheeled suitcases as they went. Announcements spilled from the Tannoy, but Jack ignored them. There was only one place he was going. He took the stairs two at a time, leaving Ruth in his wake. The platform was dotted with travellers all inspecting tickets or departures boards. None of them saw the young woman in the nightgown walking along the tracks.

'Hannah!' Jack shouted.

A few eyes turned and murmurs became gasps as the passengers turned to see Jack sprinting along the tracks towards Hannah. The question now was who would reach her first, Jack, or the distant train passing through the station at full speed.

Gasps turned to screams as both drew closer. Hannah strolled alongside the tracks, the train closing at tremendous speed, thundering towards her, horn screaming. Hannah casually crossed from the space beside the track directly into the train's path.

'Hannah!' Jack screamed again; voice drowned by the heavy metal death bulleting towards him.

The sunlight shone through Hannah's gown for a second, outlining her shapely legs before the light was blocked by the train. The brakes were screeching but even if they'd been applied half a mile ago, it would have made no difference. All Jack could hope was that he was close enough.

He dived and braced himself for that split-second of agony which meant death. The high-pitched squeal of brakes drowned any screams that came from the platform and he grabbed Hannah and rolled, hoping the next thing he felt was the rough stones at the other side of the track.

2

Jack landed hard, and the screaming train slid past endlessly. Jack had to look down into his arms to make sure. Hannah was there. The jolt of the landing knocked Hannah from her trance, and she screamed and struggled, kicking out perilously close to the wheels flying by. Jack held tighter until the train was gone and the cheers and relief from the platform hit.

'Hannah!'

Ruth was running towards them, a slew of guards and railway employees in her wake. She grabbed Hannah tightly, looking at Jack over her shoulder. Her eyes were burning with rage.

'I want someone to answer for this.'

Jack knew exactly how she felt. Someone was responsible for this and they were going to get away with it.

Employees helped Hannah to her feet before guiding them back onto the platform. Ruth looked back at Jack. Jack nodded. Walkie-talkies barked as soon as the tracks were clear, giving the green light for trains to start running again. Jack looked up to see a familiar face striding along the platform towards him. An old colleague from his days on the Force.

'Gordon Foy. This is a bit below your pay grade, isn't it?'

Foy was older than Jack, a long-time copper with little patience for nonsense. Foy was only around for six months before he got promoted out and transferred. The last place Jack expected to see him was here. When they were working together, Foy always saw Jack as a maverick, an upstart, but there was always respect. On his last day, he'd taken Jack aside and told him if he played ball, that the sky was the limit for him. Jack just hoped Gordo remembered that part.

'Jack Talbot. So this is what you get up to now you've quit the force.'

Jack shrugged. 'It's not always this exciting.'

A few minutes later they were alone in a waiting room, two uniforms guarding the doors making sure no one else came in.

'What are you mixed up in here, Jack?' Foy was stood hands on hips, wrinkles etched on his forehead.

'She's a client. I've gone private now.'

THE VANISHING OF FLIGHT 187

'A client?'

'Well, the sister. My work's done on the case.'

'What was "the case", exactly?'

Jack was reluctant to talk for fear of dropping the Drapers in the shit, but Foy knew something. He had to keep him talking.

'Something weird is going on here Gordo. I've had people trying to kill me, all over a girl who seems intent on finishing the job herself. Not a lot makes sense.'

'Well, if *you've* got any sense, you'll step away from this.'

It was Jack's turn to frown. 'Gordon Foy. You've never backed down from anything in your life.'

'I didn't get this far by not learning to pick my battles, Jack.'

'That sounds like a cop out. You used to have a pair of bollocks. What happened to you?'

Foy grabbed Jack by the collar and shoved him against the window. The rattle led to one of the uniforms outside turning his head, before looking away again.

'Listen Jack. This isn't a silly little game.'

'My friend is in the hospital,' Jack shouted. 'They shot him. Don't tell me it's not a fucking game. I'm well aware. Tell me something, Gordo. Give me a reason to step away, because at this moment in time, I'm ready to beat the shit out of something.'

Foy's grip released and he paced away.

'I'm only in here as a friend,' he said. 'I'm trying to warn you.'

'Of *what*, for fuck's sake?'

Foy turned and eyed Jack.

'This stays in this room.'

'Of course. Just tell me what's going on.'

He pulled a folded sheet of paper from his inside pocket. 'Hannah Draper is on a list. Her name and a bunch of others. It's only gone out to the higher-ups. Anything happens with anyone on this list and it gets kicked straight upstairs.'

'Above you?'

'*That's* what you're dealing with.'

Jack reached into his own pocket. 'This list of yours. Is Nicola Lutton on it?'

Foy unfolded the paper and scanned the list with his dark eyes. He stopped and looked up.

Jack unfolded his passenger list and started to read from the top. 'Paul Ashcroft. Eric Barnes. Amy Barnes. Steven Fletcher.'

Gordon went white and snatched Jack's list. 'Where did you get this?'

'Keep it.' Jack pulled the other sheet of paper from his pocket. The sketch of the military man from the airport. 'You know who this is?'

Foy stared and shook his head. Jack believed him. He turned and pushed the door open and stepped out onto the platform. The excitement from earlier had faded and things were already back to normality.

Foy shouted after him, 'Where are you going, Jack?' his booming voice echoing from the waiting room.

Jack folded the sketch up and stuffed in into his pocket. 'To get some real answers.'

'Jack!' Foy shouted, voice no longer echoing, 'Don't say I didn't warn you.'

Jack never looked back.

3

Adam Shepherd was driving home from the office, and for the first time in a week, he had a smile on his face. Whoever Adrian Grieve was, Adam had listened to him and just like he'd promised, his problems had gone away. The airline was no longer front-page news (a foiled terror plot had stolen that particular honour) and despite the initial slump, the share price was moving back to where it had been before the incident and looked like it might continue to rise. Bookings for the flights had recovered too. Perhaps this wasn't going to be the complete disaster he'd imagined.

He pulled into the driveway and parked up. At this time of day, he'd have the place to himself. He could whip up a spot of lunch and watch the Amazonian rain forest documentary he'd recorded.

His keys slid to a stop in the middle of the island in the kitchen and he went straight to the fridge for a drink of juice. He opened the door and stopped dead. There were voices coming from the living room. Slowly, he pushed the fridge door closed and cocked his head in the direction of the voices. The living room. The burglar alarm hadn't gone off. Who could get in without tripping it?

Grieve.

He edged towards the sounds, phone in hand, ready to hit dial on the 999 call. Why would Grieve be here? He'd done everything he'd asked. No news about what really happened to the flight had got out, Christ, no one was even talking about it anymore. At the doorway, he stopped and took a deep breath, before leaning around the corner.

'Bloody hell.'

The room was empty; the television was on. He walked into the empty room, put his phone down and picked up the remote. The screen went blank and he headed back for the kitchen.

Lunch would be nothing fancy, but the thought of the Spanish omelette was making his mouth water. He grabbed the potatoes from the fridge and closed the door. He reached for the radio but his hand stopped in mid-air. A chill crawled up the length of his back. There were voices coming from the living room. The television was back on.

He patted himself down, searching for his mobile. It was in the living room. He'd put it down when he picked up the remote. He grabbed a knife from the drawer and edged towards the voices.

'I'm armed,' he shouted, trying to hide the tremble in his voice.

His calls were met with silence. Silence only broken by the canned laughter from the television. It was the news before. Now it was a sitcom.

Someone's changed the channel.

His heart thumped in his chest and his palms were slick

THE VANISHING OF FLIGHT 187

with sweat as he stepped silently towards the living room. His grip tightened on the knife as he stood in the doorway, ready to burst in. Again, he drew a deep breath, his pulse thudding in his ears, and leaned around the corner. The room was empty. He reached down for the remote again and turned the TV off. At the same moment the TV fell silent, a loud blast of rock music came from the kitchen.

Adam screamed and dropped the knife. His eyes fell to the arm of the chair where he'd left his mobile.

'Shit.'

It was gone.

'Adam!' Someone shouted from behind.

He yelled and turned and before he could react, he was pushed back onto the settee. The intruder had hold of him by the scruff of the neck and he could feel the cold point of the knife pressed against his jugular, pressure rising and falling with his pulse.

'Oh shit don't kill me don't kill me.'

He could only see his eyes through the ski mask, but the intruder looked crazed, blue eyes wild, ringed with dark circles from a lack of sleep. He said nothing, only stared.

'Look, there's money. In the house. I can get it.'

'Shut up.'

Adam held his hands up, 'Please. I've got a family.'

'If you don't do as you're told, they're going to miss you.'

Adam whined. 'Please, tell me what you want. We can sort all of this out.'

The man let go of his collar. 'Scream or speak when I

don't ask you to, you'll die of blood loss before the ambulance gets here. Understand?'

Adam nodded.

'I've got one question. Answer it truthfully, and you live. You never see me or hear from me again. Ever. And I'll know if you're lying. Are we clear?'

Adam nodded.

The man pulled a folded piece of paper from his pocket and opened it. It was a sketch of Adrian Grieve.

'Who is this?'

'Oh, no,' he said.

'Who is it?'

'I can't tell you.'

The man took a step closer and raised the knife. 'What?'

Adam Shepherd's words came out with tears. 'I can't. I can't. He said if I ever mention his name, he'll ruin me. My business.'

The intruder took another step closer, 'Well that was his mistake in telling you.'

'Please he'll ruin me.'

The cold point of the knife was pressed back against his throat.

'Which seems more urgent?'

Adam nodded. 'Okay. Okay. I'll tell you. It's Adrian Grieve.'

'Louder.'

He shouted, 'Adrian Grieve.'

The man stepped back. 'Good. Now, if you go to the police, I'll come back. Be a good boy, and we never see each other again. Have I made myself clear?'

Adam nodded.

'And don't bother checking your cameras. They're off.'

The intruder turned and walked away, throwing the knife to the floor, and opening the front door. He turned and stared at Adam, removing a latex glove before disappearing into the garden.

4

Jack pulled off the ski mask as he tore along Adam Shepherd's gravel drive, only slowing to a walk when he reached the street. He reached into his pocket and removed the phone.

'Did you get that?'

Ruth Draper replied.

'Adrian Grieve.'

'And Damien gave you the full instructions?'

'Yes. I know what to do.'

Jack nodded. 'Good. How's Hannah?'

'She's okay. For now. They're keeping her under observation at the hospital.'

'It's going to be okay, Ruth. Try not to worry.'

Jack was already at his car. He glanced back at Adam Shepherd's house, but there were no signs of movement. His threats had been taken seriously.

'Speak to you soon,' he said, before hanging up.

Part one was over. He'd got a name. Adrian Grieve. Now all he needed—

His phone rang.

'Damien?'

'Jack. I need to speak to you.'

'Did you manage to sort everything?'

There was silence. Had he fucked this up?

'Damien?'

'I can't talk now. Can you meet me?'

This was bad. Jack wondered if he'd made a mistake heaping so much responsibility on the young journalist. 'Back at the flat?'

'No,' Damien replied. 'It has to be somewhere private. I'm scared, Jack.'

Grieve had got to him. If Damien insisted on choosing the meeting place, it was big trouble.

'Somewhere public would be better, Damien, surely.'

'No. Too many people. They shot at you in broad daylight.'

If Jack was going to meet somewhere secluded, he was going to choose the spot. He recalled the night in the rain. The first time he was chased. 'The industrial estate. The old brick factory.'

After the briefest of pauses, Damien replied.

'Okay. Thanks Jack.'

THE VANISHING OF FLIGHT 187

The industrial estate was deserted when Jack arrived. On the way he'd passed the odd car or van, but once he pulled onto that space in front of the old factory, there was not a soul in sight. Jack parked and called Damien's mobile, but it went to voicemail. Jack got out of the car and looked around. If Damien was here, he was in the old factory building.

Jack heard a voice, faint, distant. It was Damien. And it was coming from inside.

'Damien?'

'Jack! In here!'

Jack stared at the old factory building. Huge double doors, big enough for lorries to enter with a smaller, man-sized door cut into the peeling red paint. Smashed windows. Tall shoots of green grass sprouting at intervals around the walls. He walked towards the factory, glancing left and right, preparing for the ambush. He'd reached the doors, but no ambush came. Jack placed a hand on the rough wood and pushed. It swung open and hit the back of the big door with a thud that echoed through the old building.

'Jack. I'm sorry.'

Damien. Bruised. Bloodied. Bound to a chair in the middle of that cavernous space. Jack wanted to rush to his aid, even though he knew it was a trap. Before he could move, a blow struck the back of his head and darkness fell as Jack fell. On that endless slump to the ground, he turned. Then everything went black. The last thing he saw was Adrian Grieve.

5

The fog of unconsciousness drifted away, and Jack's eyes opened. He flinched as pain flared into his brain from the bright daylight still burning through the small factory window. Jack wanted to shake the mist from his mind but doing so might have rendered him unconscious again. In the shadows ahead he saw a shape and remembered what it was. Damien. Still tied to a chair and now gagged. Jack realised his own hands were bound. The only thing in his mouth though, was dryness.

Jack steadied his gaze and his eyes settled on Damien's swollen face. Damien had been giving them some smart talk, no doubt. Now he was out cold. Grieve had interrogated him, but what had he given up?

Nothing. Nothing, or we'd both be dead.

From the dark recesses of the warehouse, the clip of hard soled shoe echoed. It was Grieve.

'Wow. You *do* do your own dirty work. Shouldn't you have henchmen for something like this?'

Grieve smiled back, 'Austerity, old boy. I did have a couple of men. Haven't heard anything from them since this morning. You wouldn't know anything about that would you?'

Jack said nothing.

'How is your friend Dr Cross, by the way?'

Jack strained against the ropes, 'You bastard. I'll fucking have you.'

'Shh, shh. Quiet down, old boy. Don't want to strain yourself.' Grieve was grinning a grin he'd been working on for years. The arrogant smirk of a man who knows he's untouchable. 'You'll do yourself a mischief. Like your friend Damien here.'

Damien groaned at the mention of his name, his head lolled from one side to another. He was coming to. There'd be a shitload of pain waiting for him when he did.

'Why are you killing everyone, Grieve?'

Grieve's eyebrows raised at the mention of his own name, 'You have done your homework. Impressive. And I'm not killing everyone. Just the mouthy ones.'

'Sean didn't deserve that. You could have warned him.'

Grieve smirked again. 'Not everyone heeds warning, Mr Talbot. Besides, if the truth got out...'

'So the passengers, you'll kill them all?'

He chuckled. 'I won't have to do anything to them. They'll do that themselves. Or lose their minds. Either way, nobody will find out the truth,' he shrugged. 'So that just leaves the loose ends...'

Grieve reached into his inside pocket, his hand came back out, it was holding a gun.

'...Ruth Draper. Dr Cross. And you two.'

'What about the passengers? They can be saved!'

'My dear boy. Saved? By who? You?' he laughed again, his face twisted into a condescending sneer.

Jack's body trembled, and his jaw clenched. But he couldn't let Grieve see his fury. Instead Jack worked at the binding on his hands. All he seemed to be doing was burning the rough rope further into his wrists. He needed a little more time. It was still light, which means he wasn't out cold for too long, but Grieve was still here, so...

Damien moaned and his head straightened.

Jack drew a deep breath and composed himself. He eyed Grieve. 'So what was it? You said if the truth got out... What would be so terrible if it got out?'

'I'm sure you have your little theories,' Grieve scoffed. 'I shan't give you the pleasure of confirming or denying. You'll go to your grave never knowing the truth. I will say this though. You've impressed me Mr Talbot. I just wanted to meet the man who didn't back down - face to face. And I must say, it's been an absolute treat.' He lifted the gun and pressed the barrel into Damien's temple, 'But now, I'm bored.'

'No!' Jack screamed.

'Do you have anything to say to your annoying little friend here, before he goes?'

'Wait!' Jack yelled, hoping to stop the wheels turning.

But Grieve had other ideas.

He raised the hammer of the gun. A pointless exercise which did nothing other than drag out the horror of Damien's impending death. And Grieve knew it. 'No. I won't wait. As much as you'd like it to be, this isn't some James Bond story where the hero is spared by yapping and—'

And then, just as Jack had given up hope, a sound echoed through the warehouse. A song about Grandma's setting flags on fire.

Damien's ringtone.

Grieve turned to face the shadows. 'Is that *Iko Iko*?'

The shadows answered. 'Sounds like it.'

Jack smiled.

'You might want to take that.'

6

Grieve nodded and his minion stepped from the shadows to fish Damien's phone from his pocket.

'Hurry up, for God's sake... That fucking song.'

Damien was sitting up now, smiling at Jack. The minion handed the phone to Grieve who answered the call.

'Yes? Oh, a video. That's nice.'

A female voice spoke. It was Ruth. 'This is a list of all the passengers on Flight 187. My sister is one of them. Some of them have taken their own lives...'

'Ruth, is that you?' Grieve asked.

Ruth continued without missing a beat. 'The truth about what really happened to Flight 187 is being covered up. Powerful people don't want you to know. This is a sketch of the man being paid to hush it all up...'

She held up Cross's sketch.

'This is the man being paid to bury the truth. His name is Adrian Grieve...'

Grieve's brow furrowed.

'If Jack Talbot and Damien Spade are not at the police station in half an hour, this information goes public...'

...The truth about what *really* happened to Flight 187.

You have thirty minutes.'

She ended the call. Grieve turned to Jack, still frowning. Then the frown dissolved and Grieve started to chuckle. The chuckle became a laugh, and then a howl and the minion joined in. Damien's eyes filled with fear.

Grieve finally composed himself and turned to Jack.

'Ruth Draper. She's been through so much. Looking after her poor sister. And didn't she try to kill herself? So sad. A tired, grieving witness. One single, solitary witness. No one will believe her. Jesus, Jack—'

Another sound echoed in the warehouse. Grieve's smile vanished. This time, it was a factory-installed ringtone. Without prompting, the minion loomed over Jack as he plucked the mobile from his pocket. Unknown caller. Grieve waved the minion towards him who handed over the phone.

Another female voice spoke. But it wasn't Ruth.

'This is a list of the passengers on Flight 187. My brother is one of them...'

She held up a pencil sketch.

'This is the man being paid to bury the truth. His name is...'

Adrian Grieve whipped his head up from the screen and glared at Jack.

'...if Jack Talbot and Damien Spade are not at the police station in half an hour...'

Grieve cut the call off. He opened his mouth to speak, but before he could start, *Iko Iko* blasted from Damien's phone.

This time a man spoke. 'This is a list of the passengers on Flight 187—'

That was as far as he got before Jack's phone started to ring.

'What do you think Grieve? Is *that* enough?'

Grieve's arrogance had melted away. Jack saw his eyes flickering as he scanned his memory, looking for the moment his hubris had caught up with him. If he didn't know him better, Jack might have felt sorry for Grieve in that moment. Grieve nodded and the minion took the phone over to Jack and answered the call for him.

'This is a list...'

'It's Jack Talbot here. That'll be fine thanks, I think he's got the message. If you could call all of the others,' Jack made sure he was looking straight at Grieve. 'Tell them their calls won't be necessary. Be sure to thank them for their time.'

The call ended. Jack glanced at Damien. He looked like a man who knew they'd dodged a bullet, quite literally.

'You know, if you got on the phone now and got hold of Adam Shepherd, you could probably get him to stop his press conference... If you hurry.'

Grieve gestured for his henchman to make the call.

'Before you go...' Jack shouted after him, '...could you cut me loose? Old sport.'

7

Jack glared at Grieve. He was going to enjoy this.

'When I walked in here and I wasn't killed straight away, I knew we were going to be fine. You didn't want to meet me face to face. You hate doing the dirty work. You think it's beneath you. You wanted to look me in the eyes and make sure I didn't know anything. The problem you've got, is that I know *everything*. I know about the plane disappearing completely, and not just from radar. I know about you and your little crew here... Military Intelligence, right? Oh, and I know about the hush money...'

Grieve was reddening. Jack knew he couldn't push too far, but that wasn't going to stop him from enjoying himself.

'You promised to pay the passengers to keep them quiet. Very generous. Especially considering you knew that most of them would kill themselves before they saw a penny. The plan about the calls from the family members was Damien's idea. What did you call it Damien?'

'Dead man's switch.'

'That's it. A dead man's switch. So if anything happens to us, the whole dirty story comes out. The videos of the radar return, you know, the one where you see the flight vanish into thin air. The testimonies of Sean and David about being told to keep this quiet. All the more believable now Sean's no longer with us. The passenger list. The same list that was sent to the top brass in the police force, so you could cover up the suicides. Your name. Your likeness drawn by Daniel Cross. Everything. So here's what's going to happen, *Adrian*...'

Grieve was no longer smirking. He wasn't shaking with anger now. For the first time in what Jack guessed was a long time, Adrian Grieve was afraid.

THE VANISHING OF FLIGHT 187

'That hush money you were going to give to the passengers? Double it. Make sure it's enough to cover the cost of therapy and care and lost earnings. And make sure Sean's partner is looked after. You asked earlier who was going to save the other people on that list?' Jack was staring right into Grieve's soulless eyes. 'You. You are. If anything happens to anyone on that list, the family is to receive generous compensation. If anything happens to me, Damien, Ruth Draper, Hannah Draper, the security guard from the airport, the story goes out. In exchange for our health, you get our silence. Everyone wins. Agreed?'

Grieve looked down at his feet. Jack had him cornered. If the truth came out, Grieve was a dead man. His employers would have the same thing that happened to Sean befall him. Not quite checkmate, but deadlock. That was as good as this was going to get. Grieve didn't look up, just nodded.

'Now cut these fucking ropes off and let us get out of here.'

The henchman cut the ropes off Damien and he steadily rose to his feet. Jack felt the tightness of the ropes fall away and he stood. He went over to Damien, 'Are you okay?'

Damien nodded. He glanced over his shoulder at Grieve. 'One minute.'

For a second he and Grieve stood facing one another before Damien swung out a right hook. It landed flush with a smack, and Grieve stumbled backwards, before falling to his backside. His henchman took a step forward, so did Jack.

'Leave it, Barry,' Grieve shouted. 'For fuck's sake just let them get out of here.'

Damien turned and faced up to Barry, head tilted back to meet the giant's eyes. Just as Jack thought Damien would swing again, he turned away and met up with Jack before the two of them strode to the rectangle of fading daylight. Damien stepped outside and Jack turned back to see Barry helping Grieve to his feet.

'Oh, Adrian,' Jack said tone light and jovial.

Grieve looked up and Jack scowled.

'You'd better pray nothing bad happens to Daniel Cross.'

Jack stared for a moment before turning and going outside. The shadows were lengthening, and twilight neared, but this was the lightest Jack had felt in a long, long time. As they approached the car, Jack called the hospital and he and Damien awaited the news in silence.

After a moment, Jack smiled.

'Good... That's great news... Thanks.'

'Well?'

'Cross is officially out of the woods. He's awake and talking, probably pestering the shit out of the nurses. They said we can visit tomorrow morning.'

They got into the car.

'What now?' Damien asked.

Jack smiled back. 'I don't know about you, but I need a drink.'

THREE WEEKS LATER...

RUTH DRAPER WAS back at the office, and the girls were back at home. She glanced at her watch. She just had time to make a quick call before her three o'clock.

'Hi Ruth,' the voice was cheerful. Surprised but pleased to hear her.

'Hi Julian. I just wanted to check we were still on for tomorrow.'

'Absolutely.'

Ruth smiled and bit her lip. 'Good. The girls are looking forward to it.'

'Oh, *the girls* are looking forward to it.'

She heard the smile in his voice and covered the mouthpiece to hide her giggle. 'Well maybe I am too. Maybe...'

'Hmm...'

Talking to Julian hadn't made her feel like this in a long time.

'Don't get carried away mister, you're still in the spare room.'

'Objection!'

'Overruled. The court's decision is final.'

'Alright, alright. The spare room I can live with. I look forward to it.'

'Good. Well,' she said, checking her watch again, 'I'll let you get off...'

The smile was in his voice again, 'See you tomorrow, Ruth.'

There was a silence and Ruth toyed with saying more, but in the end just said, 'Bye, Julian,' and placed the phone back into its cradle.

Her eyes glazed over as she thought about what the future might hold with her formerly estranged husband when there was a knock at the door.

She checked her watch again. Five minutes early.

'Come in.'

The door opened and a man in a workman's uniform holding a bag full of tools backed into the room before gently closing the door. As he turned Ruth recognised the face, but there was something different. A goatee. Fake? For a second, her heart leapt.

The man turned and smiled. 'Ruth.'

She placed a hand on her chest, 'Jack Talbot, you scared the life out of me.'

'Sorry about that. We should be fine to talk after... you know, but I didn't want to push our luck.'

'Is everything okay?'

'Yes, yes,' he smiled. 'With me, everything's fine. I've just come to see how everything is with you. How's Hannah?'

Ruth's face darkened for a second, but it was fleeting. 'You know, I think she's going to be fine. She's getting good help. She's in the right place, and they're looking after her. We talk every day. It will be a slow road, but she'll get there. Hannah's much stronger than I gave her credit for.'

Jack nodded and smiled. 'I'm glad to hear it. And you?'

Ruth's face lit up and for the first time since Jack had

THE VANISHING OF FLIGHT 187

known her, she looked happy. 'Good. Really good. I can't thank you enough. And Dr Cross. How is he?'

'He's a pain in the arse,' Jack shrugged. 'But he's doing very well. I'll tell him you were asking after him. He'll like that.'

'Anything new with you?' she asked.

'I've got a new office.'

'Not as a repair man?' Ruth gestured at his uniform.

'No, not as a repair man—'

There was a knock at the door.

'That'll be my three o'clock,' Ruth said, standing. 'One moment,' she shouted. She held out a hand. 'Thanks again Jack.'

Jack shook her hand. 'Pleasure.' He passed her his card. 'If you need anything...'

Ruth had a card of her own ready. 'If you need a lawyer.'

Jack smiled and pocketed the card. 'Take care, Ruth.'

They got to the door and a serious-looking man and woman in business suits were waiting.

Jack turned to Ruth, 'Well, that should be fine now. Remember, if you need anything...'

'I'll be in touch,' She smiled.

Jack left and strolled the short distance to the lift. He hit the button and turned back to see Ruth showing her clients into her office. She looked back at Jack and waved and smiled, and Jack returned the gesture, before watching her disappear into her office. Ruth Draper was going to be just fine.

EPILOGUE

JACK SURVEYED HIS surroundings from his seat behind the desk. He placed the picture of himself and Jenny down and adjusted the angle, losing himself in the memory for a moment.

'Where do you want this?'

The delivery driver with the last of his boxes, stood just inside the doorway of Jack's new office.

'Just drop it there, that's fine,' Jack said rising to his feet pointing to the corner. He ambled around the desk.

'That's the last of them,' the man said in a soft Yorkshire accent.

'Thanks very much,' he nodded, shaking his hand and slipping him a tip. 'Get yourself a pint.'

'Much obliged,' he smiled and then nodded and turned to leave. 'You want this open?' he asked, gripping the doorknob in his hand.

'No, you can close it.'

He closed the door and Jack paced his new den. His desk was in the main room, with rooms off it either side, and a small kitchen to the left with a fridge and kettle. If things really took off, the main room could become the reception and the room to the right would be his office.

'Not bad, Jacky boy. Not bad at all.'

He lowered a slat on the blind to take in the busy street view below. The new office would take a little getting used to, but it was a massive upgrade on his last. A knock at the door made him jump. He turned to see a figure at the frosted glass door. He smiled.

'Who is it?'

Like he didn't know.

'It's me,' Cross shouted from the other side.

'I know, you twat, come in.'

Cross entered holding a paper bag, beaming.

'Look at this,' he said taking in his surroundings. 'Very professional.'

Jack pointed at the door. 'Got a guy coming tomorrow to do the lettering.'

'One to cross off your bucket list.'

'That's one I've wanted since I was a kid.'

Cross came over to the desk and the bag clinked when he put it down. He pulled out a bottle of Maker's Mark and two tissue-wrapped tumblers. 'Shall I do the honours?'

'Be my guest,' Jack nodded.

Cross set the glasses out and started to pour, encouraged by Jack to keep going as he slowed down. He handed a glass to Jack and raised his own.

'Welcome to York, Jack.'

'Cheers.'

The glasses clinked and they drank.

Cross looked at Jack, 'Don't suppose you've got any clients yet.'

Jack shook his head. 'Put an ad out a few days back. Now we wait, as they say.'

Cross moved to the window and lowered a slat on the

blind with a finger as Jack had done moments before.

'You know, if you're at a loose end, I've got something you can help me with...'

'Haunting? UFO? No, wait, I've got it. More werewolves.'

Cross turned to Jack and smiled. 'Haunting actually...'

The End

You've made it this far, congratulations!
Thanks for reading! Almost done...

Reviews are gold for authors!
If you enjoyed *The Vanishing of FLIGHT 187*, please rate and review at Amazon.com, it would be a huge help and would mean a lot to me!

Just one more thing...

To stay abreast of the latest developments with future book releases, why not join my mailing list? You'll even get your hands on a FREE digital copy of my gripping short story 'Infinity'!

For more information, I can be found at the following:

My website: www.marcwshako.com

My Facebook page:
https://www.facebook.com/marcwshako/

Follow me on Twitter at...
https://twitter.com/MarcWShako

Find out where it all began...

THE DEATH OF LASZLO BREYER

A **JACK TALBOT** THRILLER

A FULL MOON, AN EMPTY GRAVE,
A SERIAL KILLER HUNGRY FOR REVENGE...

"Pure spine-chilling brilliance from start to end!"

"One of those books that you pick up and cannot put down."

Former detective Jack Talbot stands accused. The grave of Laszlo Breyer, his dead wife's killer, has been robbed.

His former colleague would love nothing more than to pin the crime on Jack. And his alibi of being too drunk to remember is helping nobody.

Then a dead body turns up, with the dead killer's MO. Torn to pieces as if by a wild animal. All on the night of a full moon.

If Jack's not the killer, then he's surely on the copycat's hitlist. And he'll need all his cunning and determination as he treads the fine line between suspect and detective to catch the killer… before the next full moon.

"One of the most … gripping stories I've ever read." Isabel Fuentes Guerra, author of *The Island of the Dolls*.

THE DEATH OF LASZLO BREYER

Available now at Amazon

For more information visit: www.marcwshako.com/books

"QUANTUM LEAP MEETS 9/11."

GHOSTS OF SEPTEMBER

WELCOME TO THE STRANGE WORLD OF MARC W. SHAKO

Ray Madison is trapped in a nightmare.

Slave to the grip of alcoholism, Ray is stuck in the past, reliving the same week over and over - the week where his life fell apart. But all that is about to change...

Ray goes to bed on a normal Wednesday evening, but the next morning what awaits him is far from routine. Thrown back in time with no explanation, horrified Ray discovers the date: September 6th, 2001.

Faced with the worst week of his life all over again and scrambling for answers, with only the mysterious stranger Charlie for help, Ray is trapped in a race against time, with terror fast approaching.

The clock is ticking...

GHOSTS OF SEPTEMBER
is out now!

For more information visit:
http://www.marcwshako.com/ghostsofseptember.html

ABOUT THE AUTHOR

MARC W. SHAKO is a horror/thriller novelist, screenwriter, and aficionado of all things paranormal, from Yorkshire, England. When not reading or writing about the undead, hauntings, modern-day wolf-men and UFOs, Marc can be found watching football, playing the guitar with various degrees of success, or engrossed in his latest addiction – binge-listening to podcasts.

www.marcwshako.com

Printed in Great Britain
by Amazon